FRONTIER CINDERELLA
Book 3 in the Frontier Matches Series

Copyright © 2023 by Regina Lundgren

Cover Design and Interior Format

FRONTIER
GINDERELLA

REGINA SCOTT

*To all the gals who live life on their own terms—
we see you, and to the Lord, who made us
exactly the way we were meant to be.*

CHAPTER ONE

Seattle, Washington Territory
September 1876

IT SURE TOOK a lot of work to be a lady.

Katie Jo McAllister glanced around at the busy Seattle street. Plenty of menfolk were going about their business, dressed like her in loose wool trousers and a collarless flannel shirt. But every one of them stopped to doff their hats and smile as the few ladies walked past, skirts swishing and swaying like aspens in the breeze.

She lifted a hand to the slouch hat mostly covering her hair. The other ladies' hair was curled around their foreheads and piled up to tumble down behind them in heavy braids and waves. That swung too as they walked. And every feller watched them go.

None of them watched her. Most of them probably didn't even notice she was female. But if prim and fussy dresses dripping with bric-a-brac and hair hanging every which way would get Uncle Cole to see her as a lady, and allow her and Zeke to move on with their lives, she was ready to give any amount of work a try.

"Here we are," Beth McCormick sang out. Now, *she* knew how to dress like a lady. Her gown was a pretty shade of pink, with flowers embroidered all over it, and it had extra skirts front and back draped in a darker pink, with gathers all along the hem. Under a hat trimmed in ribbon and flowers, her hair was the color of the gold Uncle Cole wished he could get the stream on their claim to spit out.

Beth had insisted that Katie Jo and their friend, Ciara O'Rourke, come in to Seattle from the settlement of Wallin Landing to purchase gewgaws for Ciara's wedding, which was less than a week away. One of the other ladies at Wallin Landing, Mrs. Nora Wallin, had sewn Katie Jo a new dress for the occasion, only the second dress she'd owned in a long time.

It was a pretty dress too, made of silk, even! Katie Jo had picked out the blue fabric because it was the color of the sky on a summer's day, like her eyes. Nora had even given her two cotton petticoats to go beneath. She ought to have looked real nice. But standing in the lady's bedchamber with Ciara, gazing at herself in the standing mirror, Katie Jo had become aware of a distinct settling of her spirits.

"It doesn't look good on me," she had said.

Nora's kind face had sagged. "Perhaps more trim?"

Nora liked trim. She'd already added an overskirt to Katie Jo's dress, with a ruffle along the hem. Nora's dresses boasted embroidery, lace, fringe, and double and triple skirts, for all she lived in a house on a wilderness farm and cared for the little ones of the settlement when their mas and pas were busy.

Ciara had studied Katie Jo critically. As the proprietress of the Wooden Rose Inn and Restaurant, she dressed more practically in a cotton blouse and skirt that were usually covered in an apron. And she wore her dark brown hair either in a braid down her back or wound up around the back of her head.

"What you need," she'd said that day, "is a corset."

Katie Jo blushed now, remembering, as she glanced up

at the sign over the door of the establishment they had reached two blocks above the waterfront. Mrs. Blanchard's Selection was written in curling letters washed over with gilt. Painted on the glass window were the words *For the discriminating lady of fashion and elegance.*

That wasn't her. But that didn't mean it couldn't be her. She just had to try. Anything to help her little brother.

She pulled open the door and held it wide to the tinkle of the shop's bell. "After you, ladies."

Smiling, Beth and Ciara stepped inside.

Katie Jo followed them. She'd been to the mercantile in Wallin Landing, and she'd come in to Seattle once or twice with her uncle for some piece of equipment. None of the shops she'd ever visited looked like this one, all pink and white, like Beth's skirts. Forms shaped like a lady's upper body were covered with corsets in white, cream, or black satin, the tops edged in lace and some with embroidery along the panels. One was even scarlet! She tried to imagine herself in it and failed.

"Welcome, ladies," called a tall woman with hair swept back like a raven's wing from her face. Her dress too was covered with lace and beading and trim. "May I ask your brother to wait outside? My clients prefer their privacy."

Katie Jo glanced behind her to see what feller had had the temerity to step into this lair of femininity, but she saw no one.

"This is our friend, Miss McAllister," Ciara said, steel in her voice, as Katie Jo faced front again. "She requires a new corset."

The lady's lashes fluttered as if she'd been swarmed by gnats. "Of course. Something in a durable cotton?"

That sounded practical. Katie Jo nodded.

Beth shook her head. "Durable, certainly, but Miss McAllister is a lady of some refinement. Satin covered, lace along the top. Comfortably boned. Sturdy laces."

Katie Jo stared at her.

Mrs. Blanchard, or so she assumed the lady to be, nodded. "Certainly. This way, Miss McAllister, and we'll get you measured."

The thought of undressing in front of this lady was as horrible as getting stuck in the privy on a winter's morn. Katie Jo fumbled in the pocket of her trousers. "Mrs. Wallin already took my measurements." She thrust the paper at the corset maker. "She thought it would be easier if I just gave them to you."

Mrs. Blanchard accepted the piece of paper with two fingers, as if Katie Jo had somehow dirtied it, then studied it a moment. Her brows went up, and she gazed at her so fixedly Katie Jo wanted to turn and run out the door.

This is for Zeke. Uncle Cole is never going to let him go unless you can prove you are a lady grown.

Besides, she refused to let down her friends. She just smiled politely.

"Are these correct?" she asked, gaze now jumping from Ciara to Beth.

"Absolutely accurate," Ciara said. "Miss McAllister has an enviable figure."

"Which I'm certain you will know how to show to advantage," Beth added.

For the first time, Mrs. Blanchard's smile blossomed. "I most certainly can, and it will be my pleasure. I'll just gather some material, and we can come to an agreement on how she'd like it made."

Beth held up a finger. "Two, if you please. Long stays and short. Miss McAllister's maid has to take a day off on occasion."

Katie Jo nearly snorted. Maid. Who did Beth think she was kidding? Anyone looking at her would know she was more likely to be a maid than employ one.

"Do I really need two of the contraptions?" she whispered to her friends as Mrs. Blanchard hurried off.

"Yes," Ciara whispered back. "A lady can more easily deal with short stays when she's alone."

She wasn't really alone on the claim, but she understood. Zeke would have been mortified to no end if she'd asked him to do up her stays for her. And Uncle Cole would have told her she was being a fool to wear them, if she'd dared to ask him for help.

Which she wouldn't have. She was just thankful he'd agreed to allow her to go in to Wallin Landing for a whole week to help at the Wooden Rose Inn and prepare for the wedding. She still couldn't quite believe Ciara had asked her to stand up with her, but she would do her best to make her friend proud.

Hence the need for a corset. She'd never owned one in her life. She'd been twelve when Ma had passed, and Uncle Cole had sold her mother's clothes to help make ends meet. As soon as Katie Jo had outgrown the dresses her mother had made for her, she'd been relegated to store-bought trousers and shirts, usually ones Uncle Cole no longer fancied.

"Whole lot easier," he had told her. "You don't have to fuss with seamstresses and the like, and they're less likely to wear out or get torn. Besides, you're not a lady yet."

Ten years later, he still didn't like to acknowledge she was a lady any more than he liked acknowledging that Zeke, now seventeen, was about old enough to be on his own too. Together, she and her brother did the bulk of the work to maintain the house and critters, while her uncle worked his trap line or attempted to coax salmon from the bay. Uncle Cole had given up his own dreams to raise them. She understood the need to pay him back for his trouble. But it was time he let her and Zeke go.

She could only hope he'd be patient with her brother while she was gone. Zeke did his best to please, but it wasn't his fault he'd been born puny. Any little thing overset him. And Uncle Cole wasn't always good about standing in front of him, so Zeke could read his lips and understand what was expected of him.

The shop door tinkled again, and she glanced back in time to meet the gaze of Harry Yeager. Her heart plummeted to the soles of her sturdy boots, then shot up into her throat. Likely even he could hear it pounding as he sauntered closer.

Like her uncle, she might sometimes forget she was a gal, but when Harry was around, she was acutely aware she was female.

Maybe it was because he was such a male. That confident swagger, that drawling voice, even the cut of his mustache was cocky! That mustache and his hair were the color of her mother's mahogany chest that had come with their family all the way across the Plains, and his hair waved around a strong-jawed face with a smile that could melt butter. When those dark brown eyes twinkled, she felt warm all over. He was taller than she was, which, she was coming to realize, was rare, and he was strong enough to swing a double-headed axe with precision. All in all, a gal could go all swoony in his presence.

It had been hard enough sitting beside him on the bench of the wagon as he'd driven her and Ciara in from the Landing this morning. Facing him here? Impossible!

She whipped around, tugged down on her hat, and prayed he wouldn't pay her any more mind than usual.

"Sorry to interrupt, ladies," he said from behind her. "I just wanted to let you know that the steamship is offloading passengers. It might take an hour before I have Miss Dennison and her things in the wagon."

"Thank you, Harry," Ciara said. "We should be ready by then."

Katie Jo heard the shop door tinkle a third time as he must have left.

She sighed.

She hadn't realized the sound was loud enough to carry,

but Ciara put a hand on her shoulder, face soft, as if she'd heard the yearning too.

"You wait, Katie Jo," she said. "Harry's going to be singing a different tune when he sees you in your new dress. He'll forget all about Miss Dennison."

Katie Jo shook her head. "Thank you, but I realized straightaway that I'm not what Harry Yeager is looking for in a wife. That's not going to change with some new finery."

But something inside her pressed upward, as if reaching for the moon. Maybe it wasn't only Uncle Cole who she hoped would see her as a lady.

Harry Yeager whistled to himself as he strolled down the street toward the wharves. His wife could be coming in on that steamship. Beth McCormick might be the town matchmaker, and she'd picked out Jesse for the new schoolmarm, but Harry had something Jesse didn't.

A powerful will.

Harry considered it a blessing, even if some called it a failing.

"He's a headstrong lad," his third cousin had complained to the town constable when Harry had run away from the backbreaking work expected of him at only nine years old. "But never fear. We'll beat it out of him."

So far, no one and nothing ever had. Not the various distant relatives who had passed him around after his parents had died when he was eight. Not the ministers and schoolteachers who had tried to settle his spirit with kind words or harsh reprimands. Not the plowing, milking, and wood chopping he'd been required to do to earn his keep. Not the employers who generally saw him only as another strong back.

Not even the first friends he'd found, after joining Drew Wallin's logging crew.

"What would I have to do to convince you to let me bring home the new schoolmarm?" he'd asked his friend, Jesse Willets, last night as they'd sat at the table in the cabin they shared now that Ciara O'Rourke had turned their former home into the Wooden Rose Inn.

Jesse had eyed him. He was bigger than Harry and Kit Weatherly, the third member of the crew, nearly as big as the legendary Drew Wallin himself. Jesse also hoped to find a wife in an area with eight and a half bachelors for every unmarried lady. "Mrs. McCormick asked me to collect her."

"I remember," Harry said. He put his elbow on the table and raised his fist. "Arm wrestle you for it."

The russet-haired Jesse couldn't resist a game. With a lopsided grin, he planted his elbow and clasped Harry's hand, gray eyes alight.

Jesse was strong. Harry's muscles, honed by years of hard work, protested the pressure. His fist moved over and out as Jesse shoved harder.

No. This was his chance. Ever since his parents had died, he'd been looking for a family. He'd found one in the Wallin kin, but he wanted one all his own.

A wife, children. Home.

Jesse blinked and stared down at his arm, pinned to the table, with Harry's on top. "You won."

Harry released him, arm aching worse than if he'd felled a dozen trees in one day. "Looks like it. Thanks, Jesse. I promise not to propose until she's at least had a chance to meet you." He grinned. "But not much beyond that."

So here he stood. On the edge of the wharves, watching small boats bobbing in on the tide as they crossed the blue-gray waters of Elliott Bay from the San Francisco steamer. One step closer to having a family again.

He frowned, studying the heads in the two closest boats. All men, if those hats were any indication. Then again, he knew a female who wore a man's hat.

His mind conjured the image of Katie Jo McAllister in that lady's shop. For one moment, when their gazes had brushed, he'd thought he'd seen something like admiration in her eyes before she'd spun and put her back to him. He hadn't thought Katie Jo McAllister had those kinds of feelings, especially not toward him.

He had to appreciate her grit, though. He understood enough about what went on in such shops to know ladies were pinned and prodded every which way to fit into their dresses. He wouldn't have wanted to let some stranger measure him and possibly find him wanting. He was done with that part of his life.

"Morning, Harry." Mr. Bartholomew, the young assistant harbormaster, nodded from his booth at the top of the wharves as Harry drew up next to him. "You expecting something from San Francisco?"

Harry grinned. "Yes, sir. Miss Alice Dennison. The new Wallin Landing schoolteacher."

Bartholomew frowned down at the manifest he must have been given and scratched his clean-shaven chin. "Funny. I don't see a lady on the list."

Harry frowned as well. "Let me look."

Bartholomew handed over the paper, dark brows high and nose higher, as if he scented a story in the making. Harry ignored him to scan down the list. Not a miss, missus, or Dennison was in evidence.

"Must be some mistake," he said, shoving the paper at the assistant harbormaster. "She telegrammed to say she would be coming on this boat."

Bartholomew shrugged and tapped the pages on the edge of the booth to straighten them. "Happens all the time. Some ladies like San Francisco too much to continue to Seattle. Look at Miss Williamson. She only lasted a few weeks before hightailing it south."

Harry *had* looked at Melinda Williamson, sister to Ada, who had married the wealthy Scout Rankin. Melinda was beautiful, charming, and sweet-natured. But there had been something about her, a fragility, a fascination with her own needs to the exclusion of all else, that had kept him from pursuing her.

Beth said he was too picky, but a man had to have some standards in a bride. It shouldn't be too much to ask for one that was pretty as a picture, clever—but not so clever she'd think she was better than him—and strong, so she could help him prove up his claim. And if she could cook as well as Ciara O'Rourke, well, that would be a real blessing.

It wasn't as if he had nothing to offer in return. His claim was one hundred and sixty acres along the edge of Eden Hill, in an area that was sure to grow as Seattle expanded. His two-room cabin was about finished. All he had to do was complete the porch overhang, lay down the planks beneath, dig a well, and put in a pump. And he had a good job, for good pay, in a settlement worthy of calling home.

A lady could do worse.

For some reason, Katie Jo came to mind again. Sometimes, when he could see up under that slouch hat, he would swear she was pretty. She was clever enough to take care of herself, and she didn't act as if she was better than him. She was plenty strong. She helped Ciara clear the tables and wash the dishes at the inn. She might even have learned a thing or two about cooking.

But Katie Jo McAllister had spent a lot of time with Beth and Ciara lately. She might have her own ideas about courting and marriage. He'd tried courting multiple times over the last few years, and every gal had chosen a different groom. It was enough to make a feller wary of opening his heart.

Which made a stranger like the new schoolmarm a safer bet than Miss Katie Jo McAllister.

CHAPTER TWO

"**I**T WAS MIGHTY nice of you to buy those corsets for me," Katie Jo told Beth as they strolled back up the street to wait for Harry in the rare fall sunlight. "I can repay you from my working money."

Beth held up a hand. "No need. They were a gift for a friend." She glanced around Katie Jo at Ciara, who was walking on her other side. "I just can't wait to see what Harry does when he spies you at the wedding."

"He'll probably be too busy ogling the new schoolmarm," Katie Jo said. "And that's fine by me."

She shifted on the boardwalk, uncomfortable even though she hadn't taken possession of the fancy corsets yet. She never had liked telling half-truths. Good thing she didn't have to do it very often and usually only with Uncle Cole to prevent her brother from getting a beating.

"There's Mr. Hitchcock." Ciara waved at someone, and a gentleman angled his bay horse out of the others passing to rein in alongside them. He wore a leather duster that had earned its share of mud, as if he'd ridden far, but his saddle was tooled leather. His mount was about the color of Harry Yeager's hair, and it had a swagger like Harry too, as if it knew it was a fine figure of a fellow.

"Miss O'Rourke," the rider said with a tip of his short-crowned hat that revealed light brown hair, combed and pomaded, if the gleam on it from the sun was any indication. "Mrs. McCormick. Ma'am."

He saw that she was female? Katie Jo didn't know whether to grin or blush at the smile he directed her way. He was a handsome enough fellow, with eyes like quicksilver. And he had a nice voice too, higher than Harry Yeager's, but warm and sociable.

"Are you heading for the Landing?" he asked.

"I'm heading home," Beth told him. "But Miss O'Rourke and Miss McAllister are returning to Wallin Landing. I don't think you've met our friend, Katie Jo."

He pulled the hat from his head and inclined it. "Miss McAllister, a pleasure. Dixon Hitchcock, at your service."

And polite to boot. Wasn't that refreshing?

Ciara nudged her with one elbow.

Oh, right. Katie Jo smiled dutifully back. "Sir. A pleasure to meet you too."

"Mr. Hitchcock is the attorney who's helping Kit with his family's estate," Ciara explained.

So, that was the connection. Ciara's intended was the guardian of a darling little girl, the daughter of his late sister and brother-in-law. Everyone had been shocked to learn that baby Grace was the heiress to a highly successful company. Kit had had no interest in running the enterprise for her, so Mr. Hitchcock was seeing to the process.

"And I have more papers for Mr. Weatherly to sign, alas," he said, patting the saddlebag on one side of his horse. "Might I ride out to the Landing with you?"

"Delighted," Ciara said. "And here comes Harry."

Katie Jo couldn't help perking up as Harry pulled the wagon in beside Mr. Dixon's horse, especially when she noticed he was alone.

"Where's Miss Dennison?" Beth demanded.

The scowl on Harry's face ought to have told her the news wouldn't be good. "She wasn't on the boat. I sent a telegram to San Francisco. Someone will need to come in tomorrow to fetch the answer."

Beth deflated. "Oh, Rina will be so disappointed. I wonder what happened."

The Lake Union School had grown beyond all expectations in the last few years to the point at which the sole teacher, Mrs. Rina Wallin, was stretched thin. All the menfolk in the area had pitched in to add a second room to the building, where another teacher would take over the youngest students. The Wallin family had hired a teacher all the way from Boston Normal, where Rina had also been trained. But school was set to start next week, and Miss Dennison had yet to arrive.

"We'll find out soon enough," Harry said. He nodded to the lawyer. "Hitchcock. You heading out our way again?"

"I am indeed, and Miss O'Rourke has already graciously invited me to ride along with you," Mr. Hitchcock said with a smile to Ciara.

"Great," Harry drawled, and he did not sound at all pleased about the matter. "Well, climb up, you two. We need to get back before dark."

"Someone's grumpy," Ciara murmured to Katie Jo before hugging Beth goodbye. Their friend would be coming out the day before the wedding, with Katie Jo's corsets.

Katie Jo helped Ciara onto the bench, then swung herself up beside her, and Harry set off, with Mr. Hitchcock riding next to Katie Jo's side of the wagon.

"Shopping?" the lawyer asked with an eye to the packages stored in the bed.

"A few last items for the wedding," Ciara told him around Katie Jo. She winked at her friend. "And some last-minute things for a lady."

"Seattle is certainly coming into its own for goods,"

Mr. Hitchcock said as they swung around the corner and started up the hill. "You may rival Tacoma one day."

Even Katie Jo had heard of the competition between the two cities on the Sound. Tacoma may have captured the Northern Pacific Railroad's end station, but Seattle had the Territorial University.

"Seattle won't just rival Tacoma," Ciara said, settling back in her seat. "She'll surpass it. You wait and see."

"Is that your opinion as well, Miss McAllister?" he asked.

Nice to be included. "Seattle can grow as big as it likes," she said. "Wallin Landing suits me just fine. They have a library, post office, and mercantile."

"James Wallin stocks everything a man could need," Harry agreed, urging the horses up the last bit of steep hill. "Fish hooks, tinned goods, trousers, and shirts."

Ciara eyed him. "Some of us need more than trousers and shirts, Harry."

Katie Jo refrained from touching her clothes with an effort.

"They are practical," Mr. Hitchcock said. "Far more so than the delicate dresses some of the fairer sex seem to delight in."

She blinked at him. "That's what my uncle says."

"Wise fellow," he said with a nod. "I commend you for your wisdom as well, Miss McAllister."

Harry turned his scowl on him. "You like a gal in trousers and shirts?"

Evidently, Harry did not. A shame she couldn't topple backward into the bed and hide among the packages. But that would only draw more attention to her.

"I like anyone who knows what needs to be done and does it, regardless of the opinions of others," Mr. Hitchcock said. "Though, if more people followed that path, I would shortly find myself in need of another occupation."

Ciara laughed at that.

They turned onto the road out to the Landing, which narrowed as it left the city. Mr. Hitchcock clucked to his horse and went ahead of them as the towering trees closed in on either side and the briny scent of the Sound was replaced by the tang of fir and cedar. Shadows crossed the road, striping them in darkness and light. Bushes rustled as small things scurried away.

"I've been meaning to ask you," Ciara said, turning to Katie Jo. "Are you certain you don't want to come in and work at the inn during the week? I could use the help if I'm to open six days a week, as planned."

Katie Jo squirmed on the bench. "And I could use the money. But I just can't. Zeke needs me."

"I told you you're welcome to bring your brother with you," Ciara reminded her. "Maybe he'd like to work too."

"He can't work much," she tried explaining. "He wasn't born strong, like me. He sickens easily. And any little tumble is like to break a bone. But I'm hoping someday soon Zeke and I can both move in to Wallin Landing. Then I can work for you all week. I just have to convince Uncle Cole that we're ready."

"Would you like me to talk to him?" Ciara offered, smoothing her skirts with one hand.

Katie Jo chuckled. "Uncle Cole isn't exactly the sort you can talk to. You more have to show. And that's what I'm hoping to do, as soon as we get you wed. Once he sees that Zeke and I are grown and no longer need his protection and guidance, I'm hoping a whole lot of things will change, for the better."

As the sun slanted through the firs, Harry tried to shake off his bad mood. It wasn't Ciara and Katie Jo's fault that the schoolmarm hadn't showed. But how many gals did a man have to court before one actually stuck?

Beth McCormick had recently intimated it was more Harry's doing than theirs. He hadn't believed her at first, but lately, he'd begun to wonder. Was there something wrong with his character or his looks that the ladies naturally turned tail? He couldn't see anything amiss, and it wasn't something a man could ask his friends, much less the females around him.

As the road widened again, that lawyer dropped back to ride beside them and was soon chatting away with Ciara and Katie Jo. A man who liked women in trousers. Well, there was room for just about anything in this world. Still, every time Hitchcock smiled at Katie Jo, Harry felt as if someone had stuck a burning coal in his gut.

Why? He couldn't be jealous. Katie Jo wasn't his gal. And it was good that someone thought to praise her. From what he'd seen, appreciation was as rare in her world as it had been in his.

"If you really want to explore the area, Mr. Hitchcock," Ciara was saying, "you should ask Miss McAllister to show you around. She knows the woods around Wallin Landing well."

Katie Jo ducked her head, but he would have bet she was blushing. "Well, maybe a little better than most," she murmured. "Seeing as how I have to traverse from our claim to the Landing several times a week."

"And where is your claim, Miss McAllister?" the lawyer asked in that fine voice of his. Harry had heard visiting nobles from England talk less fancy.

"Up near Salmon Bay," she said. "Along the Outlet, the crick that runs from Lake Union toward the Sound. But don't come up that way without telling me first. My uncle doesn't take well to visitors, particularly ones he hasn't met before."

"I'll be certain to warn you in advance," Hitchcock said. "What made your uncle settle so far out, if I may ask?"

"Wasn't my uncle," Katie Jo said. "My pa and ma settled the claim. They were hoping to fish and log and send everything down the crick to the Sound and south to Seattle. My uncle came to help. They managed to prove up the claim. Do you know what that means?"

He nodded. "Your parents had five years to prove that they had built a residence or cultivated the land and resided on it for more than six months of the year. They then had to produce credible witnesses, presumably your uncle and a neighbor, who filed affidavits that they had proved their claim, resided on it, had sold none of it, and were loyal citizens of the United States."

"I didn't know that last part." Surprise tinged her voice.

He chuckled. "Well, I am an attorney."

"The Wallins had to do the same," Harry put in. "John told me. He's offered to write an affidavit for me when my claim is ready, which it should be by spring."

"Well done, Mr. Yeager," Hitchcock said. "I cannot imagine the amount of toil involved for a gentleman to go to the trouble of building a house, clearing the land, and establishing a home."

Maybe he wasn't so bad after all. "It's been work, but it will be worth it when my wife and I settle in at last."

The wagon bench shifted under him. Had someone slouched? He wasn't sure why either Ciara or Katie Jo would care. Everyone around Wallin Landing knew he was intent on courting.

Everyone.

"A wife as well," Hitchcock mused. "Congratulations."

"Don't congratulate him yet," Ciara warned with a sisterly grin at Harry. "He hasn't found his wife."

Harry urged the horses faster. "Only a matter of time."

"You married, Mr. Hitchcock?" Katie Jo asked.

And the coal commenced burning again.

"No, Miss McAllister. I find my work keeps me too

busy to search for a bride. Mr. Yeager will likely be married long before I will."

If Harry had anything to say in the matter.

"Oh, I don't know, Mr. Hitchcock," Ciara said, cocking her head as if considering him. "Fine-looking fellow like you, with a good income and a ready address, ought to be able to find a wife, even in Seattle." She slid sideways and bumped into Katie Jo. "Isn't that right?"

Harry glanced over in time to see Katie Jo wrinkle her nose, making her look a bit like a rabbit. "Courting isn't for the faint of heart in these parts."

"And there are still far more men than women," Ciara agreed. "Which means a lady can afford to take her pick."

And didn't he know it.

"And what sort of gentleman do you prefer, Miss McAllister?" Hitchcock asked.

Harry leaned to the right. It was the road. It had nothing to do with wanting to hear her answer better.

"I guess I never gave it much thought," she admitted. "I never expected to go courting."

Harry frowned, straightening. Why wouldn't she be courted? Lots of fellows would be proud to wed a lady they didn't have to pamper.

"Miss McAllister practically raised her brother," Ciara told the lawyer. "She helps her uncle on the claim, and she helps me at the restaurant and inn. I don't know what I'd do without her. Some fellow is going to be very fortunate when he wins her affections."

"I have no doubt," Mr. Hitchcock said with a smile.

Katie Jo bent forward to look around Ciara at Harry. "Can you pull the horses over? I need a moment."

"Sure." Harry guided Lancelot and Percival, the two steeldust horses James Wallin had allowed him to use on the trip, over to the side of the track. Even as the lawyer reined in as well, Katie Jo dropped from the bench and took off into the trees.

"Is she all right?" Hitchcock asked.

Ciara shook her head. "I don't know. She was fine in Seattle, and we didn't eat or drink anything there. Perhaps I should…"

Harry shoved the reins at her. "Hold the horses. I'll see to Katie Jo."

Before either of them could stop him, he jumped down and loped after her.

She'd only gone a little ways into the thicket, just far enough so those on the road might not catch a glimpse of her. Her back was to Harry, and her shoulders were shaking.

He stopped a few feet away. "You all right?"

She stiffened, and he could see she was wiping at her cheeks. "Fine. I'll be back shortly."

"You don't look fine." He edged closer. "That lawyer bothering you? I'll send him packing."

She sniffed and turned at last. Even in the cool shade of the forest, he could see the tracks of tears on her round cheeks. "It's all right, Harry. It wasn't him. I guess all the changes just got to me. Coming in to the Landing, preparing for the wedding, and a corset!" Color flamed into her cheeks, and she dropped her gaze.

"Some people always have opinions on what you can do better," he allowed, settling his boots on the mossy ground. "Dress a certain way, talk a certain way, even walk a certain way! That doesn't change who you are inside."

She heaved a sigh. "Maybe that's the real problem. I'm not sure who I am inside."

Harry straightened. "Course you do. You're Katie Jo McAllister."

She peered up at him from under her hat. "And who's that?"

He opened his mouth, then shut it again. Who was he to tell her? He didn't know her all that well. And he might get it wrong.

"I don't know," he admitted. "But from what I've seen, she's a hard worker, unafraid of stepping up to new challenges if it means helping others, and she doesn't bristle up over little things."

She glanced around him in the direction of the wagon. "Maybe not the last."

Harry grinned at her. "Well, don't prove me wrong on that one. We don't need any folks who like to bristle up at Wallin Landing." He held out his arm. "May I escort you back to your conveyance, Miss McAllister?"

Her smile lit her blue eyes, and something inside him lit as well. He was pretty sure he was strutting as she put her hand on his arm and returned to the wagon with him.

She climbed up her side, and he went around to his. Ciara looked from her to him, then settled back with a smile as well.

"I can hardly wait for the wedding," she said, and Harry had a feeling she was talking about something other than the ceremony.

CHAPTER THREE

M R. HITCHCOCK HAD been very nice to her. Harry had been even nicer. Had the world keeled over, and she hadn't noticed?

Katie Jo kept an eye on both of them the next few days as she helped the Wallin ladies prepare for Ciara's wedding. The lawyer spent a lot of time with Kit and Ciara, going over estate business while Nora cared for little Grace. Harry spent his days working with Drew and Jesse, trying to fill a few more orders for prime timber for furniture and ships before the cold weather set in. He did head in to Seattle the next day to see about the telegram concerning the new schoolmarm.

"Dressed in his Sunday best," Katie Jo told Ciara as she watched from the kitchen window of the inn.

"You needn't sound so sad about the matter," Ciara encouraged her, wiping out a cup she'd just washed. "Alice Dennison can't be in Seattle. The next steamer from San Francisco won't be in for days, there are no roads she can follow, and she can hardly fly here like a gull."

Apparently not, for Harry returned that afternoon with news that Miss Dennison had indeed been delayed and hoped to be on the *next* steamer.

Which meant Katie Jo had a reprieve before she had

to watch Harry court another lady, not that it was any of her affair.

As it was, she had plenty to keep her busy and plenty to share the work. Unlike at the claim, where she was the only gal, she was surrounded by ladies at Wallin Landing. Many of them were the wives of one of the Wallin brothers, whose parents had filed the first claims in the area.

Now the settlement had grown considerably. What had once been a big clearing on a bench above the lake had become the town center, with the school at the back, the inn at the front, a big barn to the south, and the church and hall at one corner, on a headland overlooking the blue-gray waters of Lake Union.

On its shores lay the mercantile and post office, along with a park and the library. The dispensary that Catherine Wallin ran as the area's only trained nurse sat on one side of the road leading to Seattle. She was the wife of Drew, the oldest brother and acknowledged leader of the settlement. There might not be a mayor or town council yet, but if there was a problem, everyone knew to go to Catherine and Drew.

Across from the dispensary, on a claim that belonged to James Wallin, the third brother, the Wallin brothers had recently blazed a new road, with space on either side for houses. The first two, log cabins like the ones they lived in with their families, had just been finished. One would be Ciara and Kit's home. The other was already occupied by the new blacksmith and his young son. His fire and bellows also lay along the road, the sound of his hammer ringing loud enough to be heard at the inn at times.

The Wallin ladies had all come to see Ciara the afternoon she and Katie Jo had returned from Seattle, with offers of help.

"You're busy enough that you don't need to help with the wedding and reception too," Ciara protested as she poured cider in their cups on the big table by the front window of the inn.

"You are the bride," Catherine Wallin had said from where she stood by the rounded-rock hearth, chin up and arms akimbo. "We should be serving you for a change." With pale blond hair, sharp blue eyes, and an air of confidence, she generally received little argument with her opinions.

"You've done so much for all of us," Nora had added, gray eyes misty, as she sat on one of the benches flanking the table. "We just want everything to be perfect for you." Nora was married to the second oldest brother, Simon. With gray threading through her soot-black hair, she looked older than her years.

"And we're the meddling sort," Callie Wallin had said with a wink to Katie Jo, where both were sitting at one of the other tables in the room, which Ciara used for her restaurant. It was easy to be friends with Callie, who had married the youngest brother and local minister, Levi. She was the same age as Katie Jo, she'd been raised on the gold fields so she wasn't nearly as polished as Catherine, and she often wore trousers too.

"I prefer to call us the matchmaking sort," Rina Wallin put in. "We are so very pleased for you, Ciara, we simply had to contribute." The sunny-haired Rina had come from back East like Catherine and Nora as part of the Mercer Expedition ten years ago, and she sounded almost regal, like a princess in a fairy tale. Katie Jo wasn't sure how she'd ended up married to James Wallin, who was something of a joker.

"Let us fuss," Dottie Wallin urged. Married to the fourth and most studious brother, John, Dottie had all the golden curls Katie Jo could only wish for.

And every last one of them were independent minded and fiercely loyal to the family into which they'd married. A shame there wasn't another Wallin brother to be had, or Katie Jo might have been tempted to try to win him over.

Ciara had given in to their urging, of course, so, while she worked on the inn and met with Kit and Mr. Hitchcock, the Wallin ladies and Katie Jo did what needed to be done. Dottie and Nora finished the last touches on the various dresses for the wedding, including Ciara's, which was a soft blue with ruffles along the hem and a big scalloped overskirt in front trimmed in satin. Terribly impractical for the manager of a busy inn, but no one else seemed to notice.

Katie Jo helped decorate the church and hall, the former with lacy lady ferns, pearly everlasting with its tiny white flowers like little bells, and delicate gentians with their transparent blue petals. For the hall, she and Callie draped bunting left over from Independence Day on the walls and tables. She also helped with the cooking.

"Though I'm not sure that's the wisest choice," she told Callie as she stirred the venison stew the morning of the wedding. "Ciara's the best cook in these parts."

"I can't argue with you there," Callie said, pulling a pan of biscuits from the oven. "But I agree with Catherine and Rina that she shouldn't have to cook for her own reception. She has enough to do running this place, helping Kit with Grace, and feeding the logging crew."

Ciara had first come to Wallin Landing that summer. In exchange for turning the bottom floor of the big log cabin that had been the original Wallin home into a restaurant, she had agreed to cook for Drew's logging crew. She'd recently proposed to Drew that he move his logging crew into the cabin he had offered her so she could make the big cabin into an inn, with rooms above the restaurant for travelers. Right now, there were only two rooms, and they were connected, which didn't leave much for privacy, but Kit and Jesse were already working on rebuilding the upper floor to accommodate three separate bedchambers. The three loggers were still welcome for breakfast and dinner.

As if Harry knew Katie Jo had been thinking about him, he poked his head into the kitchen. He'd already changed into his best clothes for the wedding, and his hair was slicked back from his face. He sniffed the air like a hound dog on the scent of a raccoon. "That smells good."

"Tastes good too," Callie told him. She popped up a biscuit and held it out to him. "Try it."

Katie Jo caught herself holding her breath and let it out slowly. Did it really matter what Harry thought of her cooking? It wasn't as if she was going to be cooking for him any time soon, in any capacity.

He took a bite, then ran a tongue over his lips, setting the bottom of his mustache to glistening. "Very nice. Everyone's always praising Levi's biscuits, but they'll sing another tune when they taste this, Mrs. Wallin."

Callie grinned at him. "I didn't cook that. That was Katie Jo's batch."

His gaze settled on her, and the stove's warmth was nothing to what pulsed through her. "You're a good cook, Katie Jo."

Callie smacked his arm. "Well, you don't have to sound so surprised about it."

As Katie Jo dropped her gaze, Harry chuckled. "You're right, ma'am. My apologies, Miss McAllister. Thank you for the taste. I'll be sure to have more at the wedding."

Katie Jo glanced up in time to see him leave.

"He'll be doing more than eating at the wedding," Callie predicted, setting the rest of the biscuits into a cloth-lined bowl. "You wait and see. Now, let's get that stew into a kettle to take to the hall so we can go change."

Ciara and her attendants were all getting ready in Catherine and Drew's cabin, which was closest to the church, though still a fair walk across the town center.

The sturdy log cabin had a main room with a bed set into the wall and two additional rooms off one end, one for Drew and Catherine and one for the older children. Every bed was covered with a colorful quilt that spoke of love and family.

Beth had brought out the corsets and decreed that Katie Jo should wear the long one for the wedding. She and Beth had one of the rooms to change; Ada Rankin, a friend of the family, was helping Ciara in the other. The slender, shy Ada was newly married, so had experience with these sorts of things.

Katie Jo felt funny changing with someone else nearby. Ever since she was a girl, she'd had at least her own corner to change, screened from the rest of the room with curtains on rope. Neither Uncle Cole nor Zeke would have been much help with changing, regardless. She pulled her shirt off over her head and wiped down with a washrag wet in the basin before slipping on the chemise and petticoats Nora had made for her and wrapping the corset around her middle.

"Let me help," Beth said behind her.

Katie Jo held still as the strings tightened, warming her middle, as though someone had set hands at her waist. Suddenly, it was much easier to hold her head high and her shoulders back. Beth let the dress down over her head, and the soft folds cascaded around her. Her fingers shook as she did up the shiny jet buttons on the front.

Beth was humming to herself as she settled the skirts on her own dress. "There. And now, our hair."

Katie Jo pressed a hand to her head. "My hair? Oh, I never thought a thing about it!"

"No need to fret," Beth said, returning to her side. "I have a few ideas." She then produced a pair of metal tongs. They reminded Katie Jo of what the traveling medicine man had used to pull a sore tooth from her uncle's mouth.

"What are you going to do with that?" she asked, leaning away from the forked iron.

Beth slid it down the glass chimney of the oil lamp that was sitting on a table by the bed, so the flame wrapped around it. "Curl our hair, of course."

Katie Jo fingered her heavy hair. "Never had mine curl much."

"It will," Beth promised. She pulled out the device and fingered a hand of her own hair. "Watch." She wound the hair around the iron, humming a little tune, then slipped it free. In its place was a bouncy curl.

"Well, I'll be," Katie Jo said, leaning forward. "Do one for me."

Beth did more than one, until Katie Jo's hair curled around her face and waved down her back.

"Perfect," Beth pronounced. "Let's see how Ciara is fairing."

They ventured out and knocked on the door next to theirs. When Ada called a welcome, Beth opened the door. Ciara was standing in front of a tall, wood-framed mirror that had apparently been brought over from Rina and James' house for the occasion. The blue dress flattered her figure, while the color made her dark hair gleam. Ada, who had hair closer to the color of Katie Jo's, must have also owned a curling iron, or maybe Ciara did, for the bride's hair was also curled about her face.

Beth went to hug their friend. "You look beautiful."

Ciara smiled at her, then looked to Katie Jo. "So do you both. Come and see, Katie Jo."

Katie Jo started across the plank floor, her skirts making a satisfying swishing, and her friends' smiles faded.

Beth and Ciara stared at each other. "Shoes!" they chorused.

Confused, Katie Jo lifted her skirts to peer down at her thick leather boots. "They're all I have. Won't they do?"

There was a whispered conversation, and then Ada was

dispatched to beg a pair of shoes from Nora. Though the seamstress was a head shorter than Katie Jo, apparently she had the largest feet of any of the local ladies.

While they waited, Ciara positioned Katie Jo in front of the mirror. She peered into its depths, and blinked.

A tall, statuesque lady stared back at her, hair cascading down behind, pink rising in her cheeks. She looked pretty, confident, almost elegant.

"A lady of some refinement," she murmured, remembering what Beth had said in the corset shop.

Ciara gave her a hug. "And you are, you know."

For the first time in her life, she believed it.

"Any sign of them?" Levi asked.

Harry shook his head where he and Jesse waited in front of the church. Kit was already inside, at the altar, and those who had come to celebrate with him and Ciara were seated on the bench pews.

"They must be running behind," Harry said. "Some ladies take a bit to get into their finery."

"Usually not these ladies," their minister said with a frown toward Drew's cabin. The sunlight made a halo on his curly blond hair.

Jesse frowned too. "You want me to check?"

Just then, the door of the cabin opened, and four women flew out into the clearing, their gowns as bright as wildflowers in the spring.

Levi smiled. "No need. Remember, gentlemen, we are doing this the way Beth described from *Godey's Lady's Book* and walking the ladies down the aisle. Harry, you start with Beth. Jesse, you follow. Ciara will come last with her brother-in-law Michael standing in for her deceased father."

Jesse nodded, and the minister returned to the church.

Harry bit back a sigh. He hadn't heard who Ciara had settled on for her attendants, but he wasn't surprised at Beth. Still, it figured that he'd be walking a married woman down the aisle. Likely Jesse would be walking with Ada Rankin or one of the Wallin ladies.

Beth hurried up to him and all but dragged him through the church doors before he could get a good look at the other attendants.

"We're not that late," he protested. "And they'll hardly start the ceremony without Ciara."

"Hush, Harry," she said, laying her hand more firmly on his arm. "Walk."

Painting on a smile, he waited for a nod from Levi, who was now at the altar with a nervous-looking Kit, then moved slowly up the aisle with her. It didn't take long. The Wallin Landing church was small, and only half the bench pews were filled. He spotted the red-headed Maddie Haggerty, Ciara's sister, near the front, along with Ciara's younger brother, Aiden. Ada Rankin had slipped in beside her husband, Scout. Ciara must have invited the new blacksmith, for Logan Bradshaw was putting an arm around his son as if to keep him from squirming. One or two of her best customers, like Old Joe, the prospector from across the lake, had also made an appearance. So had the lawyer, Dixon Hitchcock.

Everyone had stilled, waiting. His and Beth's footsteps echoed as they marched up the plank floor.

At the altar, he fell in to one side of Kit then turned to watch the next couple approach.

And nearly fell off his feet.

Jesse was coming toward them, head high and walk steady, with one of the most beautiful women Harry had ever seen on his arm. She had hair like honey, thick and rich, with curls that begged to be touched. She filled that simple blue gown with more curves than a mountain road. Her gaze was on her hem, as if she wasn't sure of her black patent leather shoes, shiny as glass. He couldn't be sure of the color of her eyes, but the softest of pinks was warming her cheeks.

Who was she? The new schoolmarm? No, she couldn't have arrived by now, and even if she had, Ciara would hardly ask someone she had just met to be her attendant. Was there some other lady she knew from her time growing up in Seattle she'd invited to be part of the ceremony? Why hadn't anyone ever thought to mention her to Harry?

Or was she married too?

Jesse stopped at the altar, and the beauty floated past Beth to take her place at the back of the ladies. His friend shuffled past Harry to stand at the back of the gentlemen. Everyone else rose as Ciara started down the aisle, every gaze on her.

Every gaze but Harry's.

He leaned back and whispered to Jesse. "Who is that?"

Jesse's voice was confused. "Ciara. Did you hit your head when you were working yesterday?"

Ciara reached the top, and her brother-in-law, Michael Haggerty, handed her to Kit, who was beaming so broadly he might have thought he'd won the millowner Mr. Yesler's considerable property in the lottery.

"Not Ciara, you dolt," Harry hissed. "The gal you walked down the aisle."

Jesse said nothing.

"You may be seated," Levi told the congregation.

In the rustle of cloth and creak of wood, Harry spun to face his friend. Jesse's brow was puckered.

"Well?" Harry demanded.

"That," Jesse said, "is Katie Jo McAllister. You sure you didn't hit your head?"

CHAPTER FOUR

HARRY MIGHT AS well have hit his head, for he was certain the walls were spinning as he faced the couple again. Beyond Beth, hands clasped before her blue gown, his beauty gazed at Kit and Ciara wistfully, as if she wished she were standing beside her groom as well.

His mind blanked. His stomach churned. He barely heard the words of the ceremony he had hoped to have read over him and his bride. Katie Jo McAllister was beautiful. How had he missed that? What was wrong with him?

As Levi pronounced Kit and Ciara man and wife, Harry knew what he had to do. He turned and put his hand on Jesse's shoulder as the couple started down the aisle. "Switch places with me."

Jesse shook him off. "No. I promised to walk with Katie Jo, and I will."

"Harry," Beth whispered, holding out her arm pointedly.

Harry grabbed her and tugged her toward the door.

She laughed as they came out into the sunlight and descended the stairs. "Someone's in a hurry. I wonder why."

"You know where the hall is," Harry said, turning and craning his neck to watch the door of the church. "Your husband is likely looking for you."

Jesse and Katie Jo should have been right behind him and Beth, yet other people streamed out of the church with no sign of them.

"Oh, I wouldn't miss this for anything," Beth assured him. She latched onto his arm anew. "Come on, Harry. You wouldn't want to be late for the first dance."

The first dance. Holding Katie Jo in his arms. Telling her he'd been blind, but now he could see. He let Beth tow him along this time, mind sorting through phrases, praises.

Pretty as a picture.

Sweet-natured and shy.

Hard working. No, did women see that as a compliment? Better to stick to her looks.

Hair richer than honey from clover.

Figure like…

"Find your partner," Simon Wallin was calling from the head of the room as Harry and Beth entered the hall. "This is a celebration." He set his fiddle under his chin.

Harry had been in the hall next to the church dozens of times. He'd help plane the logs that supported the structure and worked with John Wallin to cover the roof with shakes. He'd set in the windows that overlooked the forest. He and Jesse had sat in chairs watching as the students of the Lake Union School put on theatricals on the raised platform at one end, where Simon now stood, toe tapping time. Harry had always thought the hall spacious and welcoming.

Now, it was entirely too crowded, with more coming behind him every moment. He pulled away from Beth and turned in a circle, trying to catch a glimpse of those curls and curves. Desperation clawed at him, worse than when he'd been trying to escape from one of his relatives' noxious homes.

Then, a laugh bubbled up from the dancefloor, and he spotted her, preparing to partner Jesse.

A growl bubbled up as well.

"Care for a dance, Harry?" Nora asked with her gentle smile, and he realized he'd stopped next to her along the edge of the floor.

"He can't," Beth said, still amazingly at his other side. "He's waiting for the next."

She and Nora shared a knowing look.

He ignored them after that, circling the floor. Beth must have found other amusements, for she didn't tag along. He kept his eyes peeled, watching for the moment he could swoop in and ask Katie Jo for the next dance. She'd always been friendly to him. Surely she wouldn't refuse.

Would she?

His palms were sweating as the music ended. He started forward to intercept her, only to pull up short as several of the Wallin children pelted past. When he could finally move again, she was curtseying to the lawyer, who swirled her out for the next round.

Harry gritted his teeth. He stood on the side, watched every movement. She was so graceful, her skirts belling behind her like a butterfly skimming across the meadow. Why hadn't he noticed? Maybe he really had hit his head, and he just didn't remember.

Old Joe and the new blacksmith cozied up to her the moment the dance ended. Harry elbowed the blacksmith in the side, forcing him back a step, and slid into his place.

"Miss McAllister," he said, "Katie Jo. Would you do me the honor of dancing with me?"

Would you do me the honor of marrying me?

Instead of taking his offered arm, she frowned at him. "Why, Harry? I wasn't sure you even liked me."

Ciara and Beth were certainly right. A corset and a new dress seemed to have made all the difference, for Katie

Jo had never dreamed of Harry looking at her that way, all starry-eyed, like she was the plum in his Christmas pudding.

"I like you just fine, Katie Jo," he said, voice sounding a little gruff, as if just offering her his arm choked him up. "Shall we?"

The blacksmith, a handsome widower who had introduced himself to her earlier as Logan Bradshaw, stepped closer. "I believe you promised this dance to me, Miss McAllister."

Old Joe, a regular at the inn, shoved him in the gut. "I saw her first."

"Gents!" Katie Jo said, holding up one hand as Mr. Bradshaw glowered at the grizzled prospector. "There are lots of dances. I'll do my best to get to each of you."

"Not if I have anything to say about it," Harry said, and he grabbed her hand and pulled her out onto the dancefloor.

Katie Jo tugged out of his grip. "Don't you get all bossy on me, Harry Yeager. You don't own me."

Immediately, he ducked his head, but not before she saw red blaze in his cheeks. "You're right. I don't. But I have too much experience with losing pretty gals to let another man steal a march on me this time."

Pretty gals. Like she was among them.

She was trying to grasp the astonishing statement when the music started, and Harry took her hands in his.

Her mother had taught her to dance when she was a girl. They'd swing around the yard to her mother's hum and laugh over their stumbles. Sometimes Pa would join in. He'd look at Ma nearly as tenderly as Harry was looking at her. One glance in those warm brown eyes, and she nearly stumbled.

So, she tried not to look overly long. Plenty of other folks to look at—the ones they were dancing with, taking hands all around; the ones watching from the side.

Beth and Ciara, who were now standing along the wall with their husbands, sent her grins. Beth went so far as to wiggle her fingers at Katie Jo as if to say she'd told her so.

Well, she had. Katie Jo hadn't believed her. She still couldn't help wondering if this was all a dream and she'd wake up back in her flannel shirt and trousers.

The moment Simon Wallin finished his piece with a flourish and lowered his bow, Mr. Bradshaw and Old Joe swarmed her like someone had kicked a hive of bees. Voices called, entreating, wheedling.

Harry threaded his arm through hers and bent closer, breath a caress against her cheek. "Don't you listen to any of them, Katie Jo. I aim to prove I'm the only man for you."

That sounded suspiciously like a proposal. A shiver tickled her back. Could she really walk down the aisle like Ciara to face a man who looked at her the way Kit had his bride—like she was the finest gal in all creation and he was awed God had given her into his care? Could Harry be that groom?

"Sorry, gents," she said, pasting herself next to him. "This dance is taken."

Their groans and protests accompanied the music as it started up again.

"You mean that?" she asked him as they took their places in the line for a country dance.

"Every word," he promised.

"I bet you said that about Ciara," she pressed, though the thought dug a hole in her heart. "And about that new schoolmarm."

"Ciara's married," he pointed out, offering her his hands. "And the new schoolmarm isn't here."

Yet.

But she knew he was right. Tonight, in this hall, against all odds, she was the prettiest gal in the room. Why not enjoy it? Tomorrow she'd probably be back to plain old Katie Jo McAllister again.

So she danced with Harry, and she danced with Harry. And when she needed to catch her breath, he escorted her to a bench along one wall. She took a seat beside Dottie Wallin, who offered her a smile as Harry hovered like a crow looking out for its next meal.

"Watching you dance is the next best thing to dancing myself," Dottie said, laying a hand on her belly, which was pushing up out of the cotton print dress.

"You'll be dancing yourself in another month or so," Katie Jo said with an answering smile. "Would you like something to eat?"

"I'll fetch you both a plate," Harry volunteered. He took two steps, then turned to Dottie and held up one finger. "Don't give her away to anyone else while I'm gone."

Katie Jo shook her head as he strode off. "Give me away?"

Dottie patted her hand. "He's protective. I've always admired that about Harry Yeager." She shifted closer to Katie Jo, until their skirts brushed. "But he can be a little too protective. Don't be afraid of warning him off."

"I won't," Katie Jo promised her. "I seem to recall hearing that Harry courted you once."

"Yes, but we would never have suited. And I fear my heart was already taken." Her smile broadened as her husband approached. Most of the Wallin kin had blond hair and deep blue eyes, but John Wallin's hair was a reddish brown and his eyes were a deeper green than Zeke's. He took his wife's hand and bowed over it as if he were still courting her.

"I have it on good authority that the next dance will be a stately waltz," he said. "May I have the honor, milady?"

"Always," Dottie said, rising. They strolled off, arm in arm.

As the first notes sang from the fiddle, more married folks ventured onto the dancefloor—Catherine and Drew; Rina and James; Beth and her husband, Hart McCormick; Maddie and Michael Haggerty; Ciara and Kit; and Ada and Scout Rankin. Gazes entwined, fingers held softly, as they twirled around the room, skirts belling.

Katie Jo plucked at the folds of her fancy dress. Could that be her five years from now, gazing into the eyes of the man she loved?

Harry plopped down beside her and offered her a plate and fork. "I wasn't sure what you liked, so I got you a little of everything."

The stew had run into the biscuit, but at least the cake and cookies were high and dry. She set to with a will, only to realize that Harry was watching every bite.

She hastily swallowed. "What?"

He grinned. "Nothing. You're just so pretty you take my breath away."

And what was she supposed to say to that?

Old Joe sidled over. A grizzled prospector, he had always been polite to her at the inn whenever he paddled over for dinner. "What about the next dance, Miss McAllister?" he asked, lined face cracking in a grin.

She set aside the plate, but Harry stood and put himself between her and the old-timer.

"Afraid this one's taken," he warned.

Old Joe leaned around him to glance at Katie Jo. "That so?"

Harry turned, gaze pleading.

"I guess so," Katie Jo told the prospector. "Soon as I finish my victuals."

Old Joe huffed.

So she danced with Harry some more. Really, it was no imposition. He was strong enough to twirl her around, agile enough to keep up with the music dance after dance. She couldn't remember the last time she'd felt so light, like she was dancing on air.

"My turn," Deputy McCormick said as they finished another country dance. "Beth needs your help at the refreshment table, Yeager."

She thought Harry might argue, but he sized up the deputy from his short-cropped black hair to his tooled leather boots, then nodded and strode off to the table by the windows, where he commenced pacing back and forth behind the punch bowl as the deputy danced with her.

"Seems you have Beth worried," he commented as they swept past Simon. The Wallin brother continued to play, but strands were starting to fray from his bow, and the music was slowing again.

"Worried?" Katie Jo frowned at her friend's husband. "Why?"

"All kinds of rules for gals, it seems." He shook his head as if he thought them all foolishness. "Beth tells me you're only allowed two dances with one man."

"Says who?" Katie Jo asked him.

He shrugged. "*Godey's Lady's Book*, most likely. It comes just short of the *Holy Bible* and Washington Territorial law as far as Beth's concerned. She would have explained the matter to Yeager, but she didn't think he'd listen to her."

Probably not. "But what if I like one feller over another?" she protested. "What if one looks at me all hungry-like, as if I was the last piece of meat in the pot, and I prefer a gentleman?"

"Refuse one, refuse all," Hart told her. "At least, that's what Beth says. Me? I dance with whomever I please. But no one's going to question my reputation."

Not with that steely-eyed scowl, they wouldn't, especially with the badge pinned to his waistcoat and the gun at his hip.

Surely the Wallin women would never judge her. Would the other gents begging for a dance complain to their friends about her scandalous ways?

Not even a lady one whole day, and already she might be the center of gossip. That did not bode well for convincing Uncle Cole to let her and Zeke go.

CHAPTER FIVE

"WHY'D YOU SET your husband on Katie Jo?" Harry demanded, glancing at Beth, where she was taking her turn presiding over the punchbowl. As at other local celebrations, the married ladies were working together to make sure Old Joe didn't spice the fruit juice with something that offered a little more kick.

"Why'd you threaten her reputation?" Beth countered, pausing to ladle up some of the ruby red punch into a tin cup for one of her nieces. "Two dances, Harry. You should know that."

"Two dances?" He scratched behind one ear. "Who says?"

"Everyone," she replied, letting the ladle settle into the punch. "Two dances says you're interested. More than two says you're intending to marry."

He straightened to his full height. "Then I've done nothing wrong."

Her eyes widened, then narrowed on him. "Oh, no you don't, Harry Yeager. I've seen you fall top over teakettle whenever a new lady appears in Wallin Landing and even one or two in Seattle. You want to marry Katie Jo McAllister? Prove it!"

He leaned over the punch bowl. "What do you think I'm trying to do?"

"You don't finish a courtship with a few dances," she

scolded. "Especially when you haven't even started one yet. You've treated her no better than a member of the logging crew up until this afternoon."

Harry turned his gaze out onto the floor. Next to Hart's dark clothing and lean physique, Katie Jo was a lush lily. "Well, look at her. Until this afternoon, she *looked* like a member of the logging crew."

"That," Beth said, "should have made no difference whatsoever. If she's good enough to marry today, she was good enough to marry yesterday, and she'll be good enough to marry tomorrow when she goes back to her trousers and flannel shirts."

"Putting that woman in trousers and flannel shirts should be considered a crime," he said. "When she's my wife, I'll see her in a dress with as many frills as one of those fashion plates you're so fond of."

"If that's what she wants," Beth said, busying herself with rearranging the remaining mismatched set of cups, borrowed from every Wallin house in the settlement. "You just keep that in mind, or I may have to apply this ladle to something considerably harder than punch."

The music was ending. He nodded to Beth, hoping she would take that as thanks, then hurried around the table and strode to Katie Jo's side.

The deputy eyed him, gun-metal gray eyes heavy. "I hear you should be done dancing with Miss McAllister, Yeager."

"I hear your wife put you up to that statement," Harry countered. "I talked with Beth. We have an understanding."

McCormick leaned to one side to look past him for the refreshment table. Whatever he saw must have assured him, for he met Harry's gaze and nodded. "One more, then."

"Don't I have something to say in the matter?" Katie Jo protested.

Harry cocked a grin. "You sure do, darlin'. Tell the deputy you'd rather dance with me than him."

"My feet hurt," she said as the deputy aimed his glower her way. "I plan to sit a spell. It's up to you, Harry, if you want to join me."

And she'd thought the corset and dress would be challenging! Who knew there were so many rules? Well, Beth. Maybe Ciara. Probably all the Wallin ladies. Which made her odd woman out.

She and Harry joined Nora on one of the benches this time. The seamstress beamed at Katie Jo as she jiggled Grace on the lap of a lavender dress with three overskirts, each edged with green embroidered hearts.

"You look lovely," she told Katie Jo. "I'm so glad the dress fit after all."

"It's very comfortable," Katie Jo assured her, giving the skirts a swish and trying not to notice Harry watching. "And thank you for the use of the shoes. I guess you don't wear boots to a wedding."

Harry glanced down at his boots. So did Nora. "Many do."

Many men did, she saw as she looked for the first time. The ladies all wore flats-bottomed shoes or short heels of leather or satin.

"Well, these go much better with the dress," Katie Jo said. "I'll be sure to leave them at the inn before I head home tomorrow."

"No, no, no, no, no," Grace said with a frown.

"Still her favorite word," Harry said with a grin.

Nora made a face at the baby, and Grace's frown transformed into a smile. "For now." Her head came up as the music stopped. "Would you hold her a moment, Katie Jo? I'd like a word with Simon, and he only has a little time to himself at these events."

"Sure." She took the nineteen-month-old and settled her in her lap. Grace regarded her solemnly, as if wondering what she knew about babies.

Harry must have wondered as well. "You like babies?" he asked.

She'd been so focused on Grace, she'd almost forgotten he was there. "I like Grace." She blew bubbles, and the baby's eyes widened as if Katie Jo had just planted a flag on Mount Rainier. Grace bounced as if encouraging her to do it again."

"She's a sweetheart," Harry agreed, bending closer.

Grace reached out and snagged a lock of his hair.

Zeke would have yowled. Uncle Cole would have yanked away. Harry winced, but he managed to gently pry the baby's fingers from his hair. But he made sure to move just out of reach.

"No, no, no, no, no," Grace complained.

"My turn."

Katie Jo could only be glad it was Catherine and not Mr. Bradshaw or Old Joe sliding onto the bench beside her. She'd danced nearly as much as Katie Jo, but every hair was in place, and her smile was undimmed. She held out her arms, and Katie Jo surrendered Grace into them.

"You appear to be enjoying your evening," Catherine said, holding up a finger. Grace latched on with one fist.

"Very much," Katie Jo said. She couldn't help but glance at Harry, who smiled so broadly she might have thought this was the best night of his life.

Out of the corner of her eye, she saw Mr. Bradshaw approaching from one direction. Glancing the other way, she saw Old Joe bearing down on her. Harry stiffened as if prepared to do battle.

Maybe it was time to bring this evening to an end.

As her other two sudden admirers joined them, she rose and held up her hand. "Thank you kindly for your attentions, gents, but I'm about done in. Walk me back to the inn, Harry?"

Of all her swains, she'd chosen him for the honor of escorting her out. His chest swelled, and he offered her his arm. "This minute. Evening, Mrs. Wallin, gentlemen."

The blacksmith nodded, but Harry felt his gaze on them all the way out the door.

The sun was setting beyond the firs, leaving the clearing in misty twilight. Rina was walking some protesting children toward home. Their voices murmured a counterpoint to the soft shush of the waves on Lake Union.

Katie Jo shivered, and Harry tugged off his coat to drape it about her shoulders. She smiled her thanks.

"Sorry if I danced too many times with you," he told her as they started across the clearing. "I didn't realize there were rules about such things."

"Me either. But I can't mind, Harry. It was fun."

Fun. He should take comfort in that, but he wanted more than fun. He wanted forever.

Someone cleared a throat behind them, and he glanced back to find that Old Joe was following them, and Bradshaw was watching from the door of the hall.

"The lady needs a chaperone," the prospector accused. His squint made the lines of his face deepen into canyons in a rugged landscape.

Katie Jo glanced back too, then looked to Harry, and her pretty face paled. "Is that another rule?"

"I expect so," Harry had to admit. "It's usually not a problem out here with all the Wallin ladies, but any pa of a girl knows to keep an eye out when suitors come calling."

She dropped her gaze to the ground. "Well, I don't have to worry about that, at least."

By tomorrow morning, she would.

Something warned him to stake his claim now. Go down on bended knee and beg her to marry him. But Beth was right. A lady deserved to know her fellow would treat her well.

So, he saw her to the inn and bowed over her hand, which set her to blushing in the light from the front window. Then he stayed outside until he was sure she was settled.

Old Joe kept him company for a while.

"She's something," he said, pausing to suck his teeth as if Katie Jo were a choice morsel.

"She is," Harry agreed.

Old Joe eyed him. "I had to fight Drew Wallin over the nurse and Minister Wallin over the piano player. Am I going to have to fight you over the dishwasher?"

"Yep," Harry said, widening his stance.

Old Joe sighed. "Figures. I ain't never gonna have a wife and home at this rate." He wandered back toward the hall, grumbling.

That would not be Harry's fate. He'd vowed it before, and he vowed it now.

But the thought only reminded him of the home he was building. Before he knew it, he was headed past Drew and Catherine's claim and behind James and Rina's, to where he'd laid out his own piece of property.

The one hundred and sixty acres ran along the base of the hill where Simon and Nora had their farm and pointed toward Seattle. Lots of good timber and a creek that provided water year round. He'd widened an existing clearing big enough to hold his cabin, a barn for the critters, and a small garden, but he hadn't had time to set up the last two yet. He'd been too busy on the cabin.

The house was squared up and solid, with a room at the front for cooking and one at the back for sleeping. The deep overhang on the front would leave plenty of room for a wide porch to sit a spell and appreciate what they'd been given. He'd already dragged out a stove that sat next to the hearth and vented with a pipe through the log wall. Plenty of shelves waited for the goods his wife would can and a sideboard with doors Drew had carved with roses waited for her dishes.

The last lumber for the porch floor had arrived last week and was stored in the Wallin barn for the moment. A trundle bed and cradle were stored there too, along with a table and chairs for the front room, ready to go into the house once all the flooring was down.

Finishing the porch would take him a week, less if he could rope Jesse into helping. Then he'd have to move out the furnishings. He'd had a mind to build a settee or a couple of rockers for the porch, but that could probably wait until after he was married. Beth and her brothers would likely be able to give him bedding and dishes to start. Ciara might be willing to share some canned goods.

It would be a fine home. He just had to make sure his wife was ready to move into it too.

So, Harry was up and shaving before the sun the next morning. The mirror and washstand had been set up in the sleeping loft, but he and Jesse had moved them to the main floor because the big logger couldn't stand upright under the slope of the roof in the loft.

"Bit early," Jesse complained, pausing to yawn before climbing down the ladder in the light from the oil lamp. "We got a big job in?"

"The most important job of my life," Harry said, sleeking back his hair. "I'm going courting."

Jesse eyed him. "Again?"

Harry ignored him. He swung out the door and stopped along the path on the way to the inn. Though it was late in the year for wildflowers, he managed to find some gentians and bundled them with fern fronds to make a bouquet.

He barreled into the inn and glanced around. No Katie Jo sat at the table by the window or any of the other tables that dotted the big room. The only sign she'd been there was the pair of shiny patent leather shoes standing to one side of the front door.

"Morning, Harry," Callie said, coming out of the kitchen. "Afraid you'll have to make do with my cooking until Ciara and Kit get back from their honeymoon in Seattle in a couple of days."

"I'm not all that hungry," Harry said, looking toward the stairs that ran along the back wall. "Do you know when Katie Jo might be down?"

"You're too late," Callie said, planting a hand on one hip. "Katie Jo's already left for home."

The words knocked the air from his lungs. "What?" he managed.

"Said she had to get back to her family," Callie explained. "She's coming in on Friday to help with the inn."

By Friday, half the bachelors in the area would have made a beeline to her door.

"Where's her claim?" he asked. "She said near Salmon Bay. That's a lot of territory."

"Take the lake trail to the Outlet," she said, tipping up her chin to the north, "and follow it to the west."

"Much obliged." He started for the door, but she called him back.

"Harry, don't you have to go to work today?"

He froze. They had three more spars left in the order Drew was trying to fill, and Kit had located them before the wedding, on a piece of property belonging to John Wallin, on the southern edge of the settlement. Drew and Jesse would be hard-pressed to take them in alone. They were already one man down with Kit on his honeymoon.

He thrust out the flowers. "When Drew comes to collect us, give him these for Catherine, and tell him I'll be back by noon. I wouldn't leave him in the lurch, but my wife could be snapped up by another fellow if I don't leave right now."

CHAPTER SIX

KATIE JO SLID over a fallen log, then stopped to adjust the pack on her back. Just because she was no longer dressed in her finery didn't mean she wanted anything to happen to it. Even if she never had the opportunity to wear the fancy silk dress again, she could take it out, touch the soft folds, and remember how Harry had looked at her, all eager and hopeful.

She tugged the slouch hat down on her hair, a few of her curls still pressed against her cheeks. Perhaps she should have waited for him to come around this morning, but she hadn't wanted to see the warmth in his eyes wink out like coals in a dying fire. Today, she was just plain Katie Jo again, in trousers and a flannel shirt, sturdy boots on her still-sore feet. She couldn't mind the ache. It too reminded her of a day she hoped she'd never forget.

A dove called from the wood, low and mournful, as if it were yearning for its mate, as she reached the twin cedars that marked the edge of the claim. Her mother and father had chosen this parcel of land in part because it had plenty of the tall, scented trees. These two towered more than a hundred feet above her and were among the last close to the house, the rest having sacrificed their lives to build the cabin.

She patted the rough bark as she passed between them,

then followed the path down onto the flat along the creek. The cabin her father and uncle had built wasn't nearly as nice as the inn or the Wallin homes. It held a single room, although it was much bigger than most one-room cabins, thanks to the length of those cedars. It had no front or back porch, merely wide stones set in place in front of each door. Instead of glass in the windows, they had paper, and her uncle had covered them with thin slats of wood, spaced enough to let in light but keep out the wind. Moss clung to the roof, and the chimney listed a little, as if trying to catch its reflection in the creek behind the house. The chicken coop, which she'd help build, looked a little less worn, its slats made of tree limbs and its roof from planks traded for the furs her uncle cured.

Her dozen chickens pecked at the dirt of the yard as she crossed. She knew each by name and temperament, from shy Sadie to fussy Fran. They trilled happily at the sight of her, and she could only hope her uncle had remembered to check for eggs while she was gone. At the moment, she couldn't catch sight of him, but that was no surprise. Every morning, he headed out to check his trap line or go fishing.

She shoved open the front door and stepped inside, then heaved a sigh. Uncle Cole just couldn't seem to keep up with the chores when she was gone. The dishes were piled in the tin washtub on the sideboard, food crusted on their sides. The fire was nearly out, which was probably good, because the kettle hanging from the arm looked like it had about boiled clean. Her canned goods were all mixed up on the shelves, as if her uncle had examined one after the other before putting them back wherever he pleased. And there was a pile of clothing waiting by the back door for her to wash.

"Zeke?" she called.

A moan from the left made her stomach clench.

Dropping the pack on the earthen floor, she strode to the bedstead along the western wall, the opposite corner from her private corner with its gingham curtain. Her brother was lying under a pile of blankets, eyes squeezed shut, as if the trickle of light coming through the window hurt.

She dropped onto her knees and rested her hand near his face, vibrating the bed so he'd know someone was near. "Zeke? You sick again?"

His eyes opened, showing a vibrant green at odds with the pallor of his skin. "Katie Jo. You're back." He pushed away the covers, and she helped him to sit.

"Was it fun?" he begged, searching her face as if he thought to see the changes in her. "Was the food good?"

"It was all wonderful," she told him, making sure to speak each word clearly. "Everyone was pretty as a picture and so happy. And the food! I brought you back a bit of the wedding cake."

She started to rise, and he caught her hand. "Maybe later."

"Stomach?" she guessed, settling back onto the bed.

He dropped his gaze. "I wasn't hungry for dinner. Uncle Cole thought it best I not eat breakfast, just to be sure it didn't come back up."

More likely, Uncle Cole hadn't wanted to go to the trouble of cooking. Pushing away the unkind thought, she put on a smile. "Well, I'm sure you'll be feeling better in no time. Can you get up? I can cook some oatmeal for you."

"That would be nice," he said.

She shook her head as she rose. Anyone looking at her and her brother would wonder how they could possibly be related. Zeke had the same honey-colored hair, but it hung limply around his face, which wasn't nearly as rounded as hers. He had their father's green eyes, while she had a blue closer to their mother's. And, even though he was seventeen now, his head only reached her shoulder, making him appear much younger.

She went to the sideboard, then reached up to pull down one of the cast iron pots hanging above it. Clumps of something red stuck to the sides. With another sigh, she set it beside the washtub with the rest and picked up the bucket to go fetch water from the stream.

Her uncle was crouched a little ways down, rinsing off a fat salmon he must have caught in the bay to the north. At least they'd have a good dinner tonight. He looked up as she dunked the bucket into the ale-colored water, green eyes bright in a face as lined and dark as cedar bark.

"They let you come back, did they?"

She hauled up the water. "I wasn't a prisoner, Uncle Cole." At least, not in Wallin Landing.

"Might as well be for all the good it does me and your brother. You see him? He's sick."

He made it sound like that was all her fault.

"I'll feed him oatmeal and dose him with willow bark tea," Katie Jo promised, grasping the handle of the bucket harder than the weight required. "But if we're too much trouble, I can take him back to Wallin Landing with me next time."

Her uncle rose to his full height, dark-brown brows coming down heavily. "So, after all I've done for you, you'd run off and leave me alone here."

She swallowed. "You could come too."

"Oh, I bet I'd be all kinds of welcome."

The sarcasm soured her stomach. "The Wallins are good people. You could find work."

He shook water off the fish. "I don't work for other people." He nodded to the bucket in her hand. "You'll need more than one of those to do the cleaning today. Bring it back out when you've emptied it, and I'll fill it for you."

At least he'd offer that much help. "Yes, sir," she said and turned for the house.

"And we need to have a talk about this work you do at the Landing. I don't see how it can continue. You're too needed here."

Her spine stiffened, and she spun to face him. "I wouldn't be needed if you'd let me take Zeke out of here. I understand you want to keep the claim. It's yours. We don't want it."

He strode toward her, and she took a step back.

"You know I can't do that," he gritted out. "You and your brother could take the claim as children of the filer, but I'd have to pay you for it at the going rate. Nothing here has ever allowed me to earn that much money."

He was so close she could feel the heat coming off his body. "You don't have to pay for it. We'll say you paid."

"I won't make you a liar." He stepped back and sighed. "Like it or not, girl, we're stuck with each other. Now, go help your brother."

She nodded, praying it didn't look as shaky as she felt, then turned for the house once more. The water slopped in the bucket with each step, but she didn't look at him again.

There had to be a way around this! She thumped the bucket onto the table beside the sideboard, then went to rekindle the fire. As it started crackling, she poured some of the water into another kettle and set it on a hook hanging from the crane to warm over the flames.

She didn't give a hoot about the claim, for all her parents were buried on it. The house was fetid in summer and freezing in winter. No matter what she did, she couldn't keep anything clean with that dirt floor. Zeke had the bed, her uncle a pallet in the loft, and she either went to sleep in front of the fire or in her corner beside her mother's chest, which held a few trinkets and finer linens than she felt comfortable using here. It had been a while since she'd been content here.

And helping Ciara at the inn had shown her a whole new world, where neighbors cared for one another and her work was not only appreciated but rewarded. Zeke deserved to see that world too.

She had just settled her brother at the table with a bowl of oatmeal sweetened with honey when her uncle stomped in from the creek, leaving puddles along the earthen floor. He tossed the salmon into the washtub with the dirty dishes before going to take down his rifle from the peg by the front door. "Someone's coming."

Zeke's spoon stopped halfway to his mouth. "Who?"

"If I knew that, I wouldn't be grabbing my gun, would I?" Uncle Cole checked for ammunition. "Leave him, girl, and get your shotgun."

"Yes, sir." She went for the gun, which was hanging on a strap above where she slept. She knew it had bullets in it. She'd cleaned and reloaded it before she'd left, in case Zeke had needed it to defend the chickens. They'd had enough foxes and raccoons over the years come thieving. But Zeke couldn't have used it this time, as sick as he was.

Uncle Cole edged open the front door and peered around it, then motioned her to go out ahead of him. She slid out and along the logs to a corner, then ducked into the crevice where the butts joined, resting the barrel of her gun on one of the notched logs. He crossed to the chicken coop and slipped behind it, earning a squawk of distress from Sadie.

She saw the shape moving in the trees and drew a bead on it a moment before a man stepped out into the clearing. Then she yanked up her gun.

"Harry?"

Harry paused as a man stepped out from behind a chicken coop that had seen better days. He had untidy dark brown hair and a full beard and mustache. The flock scurried away from him as he looked toward the house. "You know this feller?" he asked.

Katie Jo appeared from behind a corner of the cabin. Gone was any sign of his golden beauty from last night. The slouch hat might be missing, but the flannel shirt and trousers were all too clear. Perhaps he should be disappointed, but all he wanted to do was stride to her side and take her in his arms.

"Yes, sir," she said. "This is Harry Yeager. He's the leader of Drew Wallin's logging crew."

The man, who must be the uncle she'd mentioned, looked him up and down. "A man has to be a mighty fine logger to make Wallin's crew."

"I've been with him for more than three years," Harry said.

He nodded, and at last he put up the rifle. "He send you this way?"

"No, sir," he said, copying her deference. "I came to see your niece."

His head jerked around, and he stared at Katie Jo as if he'd never noticed her before. "That so?"

Katie Jo hurried forward. "I must have forgotten something at the inn. Isn't that right, Harry, er, Mr. Yeager?"

She gazed up at him so hopefully, he was tempted to agree. But he wanted her to know she had become important to him. "You did, all right. You forgot my heart. I believe I laid it at your feet last night."

She sucked in a breath, eyes widening.

"Well, then," her uncle said, "maybe you better come in and set a spell." He strode past him without waiting for Harry to agree.

"Everything all right?" he whispered to Katie Jo when she hesitated to follow.

She shook her head, but she slipped her hand into his as they moved forward. Once more, Harry's chest swelled.

Inside, the house wasn't much better than the coop. Whoever had built it seemed to have been in a hurry, for he could see daylight through some of the chinking between the logs, and the ceiling sloped in places, as if the roof hadn't been laid on square. At least the hearth was well built of rounded rocks mortared in place. The fire cast a warm glow, but the single room still seemed as dark as a cave.

It might have been the dim light that made him miss the other occupant until the boy moved. Slight and slim, he pushed away from the table to stand just behind his uncle, who had taken up his place in front of the hearth. His shirt sleeves and pant legs were too short, or maybe he'd just shot up and grown out of them. Harry remembered those days.

"Mr. Yeager," Katie Jo said, letting go of his hand, "you've met my uncle, Cole McAllister. This is my brother Ezekiel. Zeke, Mr. Yeager came to visit us from Wallin Landing. He's one of Drew Wallin's crew."

"Pleased to meet you," the boy said, holding out his hand. Harry went to shake it. It was thin, and he felt like he'd grabbed a bird's wing by mistake, but Katie Jo's brother gave him a good squeeze.

"Likewise," Harry said as they disengaged. "Katie Jo's mentioned how fond she is of you."

Pink rose in his cheeks, and he ducked his head.

"*Katie Jo* must talk to you more than she talks to me," her uncle said, settling himself in one of the two rocking chairs by the hearth. He laid the rifle across his thighs, as if he thought he still might need it.

"She's not much of a talker," Harry said with a smile her way. "That suits me just fine."

Now she blushed too. "You probably need to be leaving soon, Mr. Yeager. It's a long walk back to Wallin Landing. Thanks for coming."

CHAPTER SEVEN

W AS SHE TRYING to get rid of him? She had to know it wasn't all that long from the Landing. Harry had reached her family claim in about a half hour, according to his pocket watch. Plenty of time to build his case and get back by noon, as he'd promised.

Her uncle seemed just as eager to talk.

"Oh, I'm sure he can stay a while longer," he said, and it wasn't an invitation. "Tell me, how did you come to meet my niece, Mr. Yeager?"

Harry waited for her to sit on the other chair, but she bustled to a tin washtub on the sideboard and began scrubbing at a pot. Industrious, always. He liked that about her too.

"Katie Jo's been helping at the inn," Harry explained to her uncle, refusing to sit while she stood. "Ciara O'Rourke, that is Mrs. Weatherly now, cooks for the crew too."

"So, you admired the way my niece works," he surmised.

Harry sent another smile her way. "I admire everything about your niece."

Her back stiffened, and he could only hope it was because she was pleased.

"That a fact." Something about the way her uncle said

it made him feel as if he'd stepped off the springboard into mud.

"Yes, sir."

"I imagine you'll be disappointed to hear she's quitting her job, then."

Katie Jo slumped and scrubbed harder.

"Why?" Harry asked. "She's good at it, and Mrs. Weatherly is going to need even more help as the restaurant grows and the inn opens. Not many in these parts could step in or do the job so well."

"I imagine there aren't," he said. "Makes me wonder whether she ought to be paid better."

The pan clanged into the washtub, and she spun. "Ciara pays me plenty. And you know you love the pies and cakes she sends home."

He held up a hand. "Mr. Yeager understands me. A lady of such value should be appreciated. Isn't that so, Mr. Yeager?"

Something in him said he should argue with the fellow, but he wasn't sure why. Katie Jo was a pearl beyond price.

"I'm sure if Katie Jo could come more days, Mrs. Weatherly could afford to pay her more," he offered. "And if she couldn't, maybe those of us on the logging crew could chip in."

She shook her head at him, but her uncle rose, drawing his gaze. "I like you, Mr. Yeager. You seem like a reasonable man. Feel free to call any time."

"Thank you," Harry said, aiming his smile at Katie Jo again.

But her eyes were narrowed as if she thought it a very bad idea. He just wasn't sure who concerned her more: her uncle or him.

Katie Jo walked Harry to the twin cedars. He kept glancing back at the claim. Probably he was surprised she lived so far out. The Rosses to the west were their only neighbors, though some prospectors and trappers rowed across Salmon Bay to find their way to the cabin and commiserate on their fate with Uncle Cole. She had to leave the front and back doors open for hours afterward to get rid of the stench of cheroots.

His hand slipped down and cupped one of hers. Warmth rose from the touch, but she couldn't understand his reasoning. Did he think she needed help walking this little distance? Putting on a dress hadn't signaled that she'd lost all ability to navigate the forest on her own. She wasn't fragile.

"Nice of you to come out and check on me, Harry," she ventured, pulling her hand from his, "but you don't need to worry about me in the woods. I've lived here a long time."

"I wasn't worried about the woods," he said, gaze coming back to her and a slight frown forming between his brows. "I just want to make sure you know you can count on me."

She cocked her head as they stopped next to the cedars, the musty scent of the bark winding through the shadows. "Count on you for what?"

"For everything."

Did he think her and her uncle were as sickly as Zeke? "Uncle Cole handles most of the heavy work," she told him. "And what he can't do alone, we do together."

He drew in a breath that raised the chest of his flannel shirt. "I'm thinking I could do other things your uncle can't. Husband-type things."

Oh.

The scent of the cedars evaporated, or maybe she'd just stopped breathing. She shook herself. Just because Harry Yeager had used the word *husband* in a sentence didn't mean he wanted to be hers. She was plain Katie Jo today, and he didn't have stardust in his eyes.

"Much obliged," she said. "I won't keep you. Maybe I'll see you at the Landing next time I'm in for the mail."

He seized on the word. "Mail! I'll bring it out to you, if Drew can spare me. Least I can do." He put one hand behind his back and bent at the waist. "Until then."

Katie Jo stared at him as he straightened and strolled out into the woods. Had he just bowed to her, like she was a princess? The world must be tilting again. Just in case, she picked her way carefully into the clearing.

Over the next couple of days, she worked on getting things back to normal. She made sure Zeke had hearty food and plenty of it, smiling as he got up and started helping her with the other chores. They pulled out their mother's Bible and read some for Sunday worship. If Uncle Cole noticed, he gave no sign as he worked at straightening some nails that could be reused.

She tried the short stays Beth had ordered for her, shrugging into them behind her curtain and hooking the front closures before putting on her flannels. They made it easier to keep her back straight, but they were a bit difficult when it came to bending and such. She found if she bent from the waist, like Harry had bowed to her, she could manage.

"There's something different about you," Uncle Cole said as they were fixing the chicken coop. The recent rains had washed away the dirt at one corner, and the shelter was leaning. So were the roosts inside. Fran had clucked no end, as if scolding Katie Jo for such a lax approach to management.

Her uncle put his shoulder to the side and heaved so she could shove a slab of basalt under the end to shore it up.

"I reached my majority a year ago," she reminded him, giving the rock one last push to position it.

Her uncle grunted as he let the coop down to the protests of concerned hens now gathered at the opposite end of the run. "So you did. But you carry yourself different too."

She wasn't about to mention the corset. "Maybe I found my confidence," she said, dusting her hands together to knock off the mud. "Maybe I'm ready to step into my future."

"Maybe," he allowed. "By the smell of that coop, you better change the bedding." He headed for the house.

Whether she came at him straight or circled around, she couldn't seem to get him to face the truth. Perhaps she should just take Zeke and go, but they owed him so much, not the least of which was family loyalty. She just had to keep at it. If Harry could keep trying to find a wife under much greater odds, surely she could win over her uncle.

Ah, Harry! She couldn't count the number of times he crossed her mind as she went about her work. When she pulled the cast iron pot from the coals to check on her stew, she wondered whether he'd like it as much as he liked Ciara's. She didn't have all the spices her friend had at hand, but some late yarrow from her garden gave it a peppery flavor that made Zeke smack his lips and offer his plate for a second helping.

When she gathered the eggs, she wondered whether Harry planned to have critters at his homestead. He'd never said he intended to farm. He seemed to like chopping down trees a great deal. He must be good at it, or he would never have made Drew Wallin's crew. What would he do when he finished logging off his property? Sell it and move on to the next? Settle down as a rancher?

Somehow, she couldn't see him yearning to follow the color like Uncle Cole had. Her father had said her uncle had intended to travel up to the strikes in the British Territories, like Scout Rankin had done. Mr. Rankin had come home a wealthy man. Uncle Cole had stayed to take care of her and her brother. When she'd been a girl, he'd spent some time up and down the creek on their property, hunting for gold or silver, but he'd never found anything. Now only his furs brought a profit for trading. But at night, his gaze went all unfocused at times, and she wondered whether he was still dreaming about the gold in the hills.

She jerked upright from where she'd been pulling weeds from the garden. Was Harry that fixated on a dream too? She'd been coming in to Wallin Landing for the last five years, ever since she'd passed her eighteenth birthday, and every year she'd known him, he'd been trying to court some lady. Dottie, a farmer's daughter near Seattle. He'd poked at Ciara too just this summer, before it had become clear she favored Kit.

Was Katie Jo just another gal on his list? How long before Harry lost interest?

Uncle Cole seemed to have similar thoughts, for he spoke up as he was stretching a mink pelt over a willow frame to dry that night. "I thought we might see your young man hereabouts."

Katie Jo tried to hunch over her mending where she sat in the chair opposite his, but the corset protested. "Mr. Yeager has work to do. Mr. Wallin won't likely let him off to gallivant all over creation whenever he wants."

Her uncle grunted as he tied off one of the leather straps that held the skin to the frame. "Thought he might bring in the mail, at least."

She raised her head. "How'd you know he said he'd bring the mail? We were alone when he suggested it."

Her uncle smiled at her. "I'm learning I need to pay more attention when it comes to you, girl. If the fellers are taking notice, I should too."

By listening in on her private conversations? That didn't set right. "You taught me to take care of myself," she said.

"I can shoot, punch, and kick as well as the next man. And I can hit the mark with a knife at twenty paces."

"Better than most," Zeke put in from where he was reading at the table. John Wallin had sent up a couple of adventure yarns from the library, and her brother had dived in headfirst.

"Comes a time when a lady needs to know more than how to protect herself." Her uncle focused on the next strap.

She kept her smile from her voice. "So I've heard. I reckon I'm there now."

"Looks like it." He rose to hang the pelt up on a hook above the mantel so it could dry. "I'll think on the matter."

Katie Jo exchanged glances with her brother, who gave her the thumbs up. Maybe it wouldn't take as much as she'd feared to convince Uncle Cole that she and Zeke needed to make their own way, at last.

Harry didn't have a chance to take the mail to the McAllister claim until Tuesday. For one thing, the family didn't get all that much mail. For another, Drew was trying to bring down those spars, and Harry was needed.

But it didn't matter how hard he worked. Everything felt flat and gray. It was as if his brain had seized on Katie Jo McAllister and refused to think anything else was worthy of consideration. Wallin Landing didn't seem to notice. Life went on as usual.

Dixon Hitchcock had left after the wedding and wasn't due to return for a couple of weeks. Ciara and Kit came back from their short honeymoon so dreamy-eyed she burned the griddle cakes at breakfast the first morning, and Drew had to put Kit on guard duty rather than chopping to keep Jesse or Harry from losing a finger when he swung the axe the wrong way.

The rest of the settlement was abuzz about the first

school board election, which Rina was fixing to hold in a few weeks. Up until now, the board had been made up of Wallin family members, but as the settlement grew and more children entered the school, it seemed only right to give others an opportunity to help guide it.

Logan Bradshaw had already thrown his hat in the ring. And Mrs. Gladys Volland, who with her husband and young daughter had taken over the old Rankin claim along the lake, showed up at the inn late one afternoon close to sunset, looking for Rina so she could volunteer for the office.

"The school appears to be closed," she complained, pointing her long nose at Ciara, who was setting the table for dinner while Harry was taking a moment to warm himself by the fire.

"The teacher, Mrs. Wallin, lets the children go early this time of year," Ciara explained, laying down the last plate. "So they can reach home before dark."

Mrs. Volland raised her chin and set the curls on either side of her narrow face to twitching. "School should go on, regardless of the weather or change in the light. Do we have no policy manual?"

"I wouldn't know," Ciara said, turning for the kitchen. "I never attended the Lake Union School. I was raised in New York and Seattle. Maybe Harry can help you." She gave Harry a wink before disappearing into the kitchen.

Harry straightened away from the fire as Mrs. Volland frowned in his direction. Now that he studied her, he could see her brown hair, dressed so fashionably with curls around her face, was streaked with gray. Slender and angular, she stood as if her spine was made of iron, printed cotton skirts hanging straight and true.

"I'm afraid I can't help you either, ma'am," he said. "I came to Wallin Landing long after I was past schooling, and I don't have a wife or children."

She tsked. "It is a man's duty to marry and raise children, sir. How else are we to tame the wilderness?"

Harry barely managed to keep his smile. "A sharp axe and a strong arm help, ma'am. But I'm working on the wife."

She nodded. "Good. Please let Mrs. Wallin know I would be delighted to serve on her board. If she would call on me at her convenience, I can give her my particulars." She minced out.

"Maybe you should run for a position, Harry," Ciara said, poking her head out of the kitchen. "You have as many opinions as she does."

"And I'll be glad to voice them," Harry said, "once I have children in the school."

She'd smiled at him as if in encouragement.

He needed it. Already, Old Joe had shown up at the inn asking directions to Katie Jo's establishment. Harry had considered sending the prospector the wrong way before Ciara had stepped in and told him that a lady did not give out her home address to strangers and if he wanted to speak to Katie Jo, he should come in on Friday and Saturday night, when she'd be working.

"Don't give him ideas," Harry had cautioned her. "He'll just take the place of a better paying customer."

"If that means Katie Jo gets the attention she deserves for a change," Ciara had said, picking up the last of the dishes and starting for the kitchen, "then I'm fine with that."

Harry wasn't. He threw himself into the logging, hoping to get ahead, but he only managed a half-hour or so of daylight each afternoon, which wasn't enough to reach Katie Jo's claim and return, with the days growing shorter all the time.

Finally, when the rain poured down on Tuesday, making logging hazardous, James Wallin walked into the inn, where Harry and Jesse were at the big table drinking coffee.

"Parcel for Cole McAllister," he announced, laying a block wrapped in brown paper on the table in front of Harry. "Don't suppose anyone would like to deliver it."

Harry surged up. "I'm your man. Would you let me take Lancelot?"

James pursed his lips. Of the brothers, he was the most fastidious in what he wore, often donning waistcoats shot with silver. Today's boasted carved ivory buttons. He was also very careful who borrowed his prized horses.

"I suppose it could wait until Friday, when Katie Jo returns," he mused, stroking his chin with two fingers. "It isn't as if anyone was aching to see her."

Harry glowered at him.

"Oh, stop teasing," Ciara said, coming through with a pot to refill Jesse's cup. "He'll take any excuse."

James moved his hand up over his heart. "As would I for maiden fair. The horse is yours. Just be careful."

"As if he were my firstborn," Harry promised. "Which I may have someday, thanks to you." He clapped James on the shoulder and went to saddle the horse.

CHAPTER EIGHT

LANCELOT WAS AMONG the sturdiest, fastest horses in the area, but the path was muddy and narrow in places, so it still took Harry more than a quarter hour to reach the twin cedars that stood like the doors of a cathedral to give entrance to the claim. By that time, water was sluicing off his hat onto his leather duster, and Lancelot's black coat was slick.

Katie Jo must have heard him ride up, because she opened the door to peer out through the curtain of rain. "Harry? What are you doing?"

"Bringing you the mail, as promised," Harry said. He reached into his duster and pulled out the package, which he'd carried close to his chest. She stepped out to reach up and take it from him.

"Come in," she urged. "You'll be soaked clean through."

Oh, how he wanted to agree. To spend a few moments in her company, sharing stories, dreams. To watch her eyes light up when he talked about their future together.

But he'd forgotten. The McAllisters had no barn. And he couldn't risk leaving James Wallin's horse standing in the rain.

"Sorry," he said. "I should get back. Just know I think about you all the time. I can't wait for Friday."

She gazed up at him, rain trickling down her cheeks

and darkening her honey-colored hair. "Harry Yeager, are you courting me?"

Harry laughed. "If you can't tell, darlin', I'm doing something wrong."

Color brightened her cheeks. "I was afraid to hope. Are you sure, Harry? Because I'm nothing special."

He leaned closer, wishing he could take her in his arms. "There, we will have to disagree. But we can discuss it on Friday."

She caught one of his reins with her free hand before he could urge Lancelot into motion. The horse shook his head in protest, and she let go. "I may not be coming in on Friday, Harry, or leastwise, that might be the last time I come in. Zeke needs me."

He needed her too, and he knew another who might be just as adamant. "Then I'll have to change your mind. See you soon, Katie Jo."

She dropped her hand, and he wheeled the horse and set off for the Landing.

Not coming in. That was her uncle's doing more than her brother's, he'd bet. There had to be something Harry could do to reason with him. Maybe he just needed to hear a man's perspective.

Or another lady's.

By the time he had reached Wallin Landing, the rain had stopped, and he had a plan. He made sure to rub down Lancelot and set him securely in the barn with an extra helping of grain before going to find Ciara.

She had yet to open the restaurant to the public outside Friday and Saturday nights, so she had only to serve him, Jesse, Kit, and baby Grace that night. She was setting the table as he came in. Kit sat on the braided rug near the hearth, hands holding the baby's as she tried to stand.

"You're about to lose your best worker," Harry told Ciara.

She set the last plate down with a bang. "Harry Yeager, you didn't propose!"

"Not yet," Harry allowed, going to hang his sodden duster on a hook by the door. "But Katie Jo is considering quitting. You might want to talk to her about it, before Friday."

She went to the sideboard and began pulling out forks and spoons. "Is her brother so ill?"

"Not that I've seen," Harry allowed. "A word of encouragement from you might tip the scales."

She glanced to Kit, who swung Grace up into his arms to come join them. She sure looked like her uncle, with dark curly hair and brown eyes. She studied Harry as if wondering what he had in mind.

"I can ask Nora to take care of Grace tomorrow if you want to go," her husband offered. "But I don't like the idea of you alone on that track, and I'm not sure how Drew would feel about letting me off work so soon."

"I'll escort you," Harry offered. "Happy to help keep the inn running."

"No, no, no, no, no," Grace chanted.

Ciara narrowed her eyes at him. "My thoughts exactly, Grace. Harry is obviously up to something. But I really do need Katie Jo's help. We'll go tomorrow, if Drew is amenable."

Drew was amendable. Harry even managed to coerce Jesse into helping him at his cabin after dinner that night. He wasn't about to bring a wife home to a bed in a cabin he shared with others.

In the last week, Drew and his brother John had helped him sink a well and put in a pump. With the rain stopped for a moment, and with the last little bit of light, he was hoping to finish the porch. Already the shadows stretched across the little clearing, and an owl hooted from the woods as if protesting the imposition on his hunting grounds.

Like him, Jesse tended to work with little conversation and a great deal of production. Harry climbed up on the overhang to lay down the last shakes, while his friend set the planks in place for the flooring.

"Hand me the mallet," Harry called down.

"Sure." Jesse reached up one of his long arms. "You courting Katie Jo?"

Harry shifted into position. "Funny. She asked me that too, and I told her I must be doing something wrong that she didn't notice."

Jesse grunted. A thunk said a plank had gone into place.

"I'm not just courting," Harry protested, laying down a shake. "I'm going to marry that gal."

Jesse snorted.

Harry scowled. "You have something to say about the matter?" He gave the peg holding the shake to the roof a good whack.

"Nope." Another board thunked into place.

"Sounded like it," Harry pointed out.

"You court a lot," Jesse said, followed by a couple of bangs as he hammered in the nails. "Still aren't married."

Harry clamped his lips shut a moment. It did no good to get angry at his friend. Jesse was a man of few words. Sometimes, you had to look beneath them to see the true meaning.

"None of the gals I courted ended up wanting to marry," he explained, laying out several more of the rough cedar shakes.

"They all married," Jesse insisted.

Harry smothered a growl. "They just didn't marry me. This time will be different."

"Why?"

He rocked back on his heels. It was a fair question. What made him think Katie Jo would look on his suit more favorably, when the rest of the bachelors in the area would soon discover how sweet and pretty she was? She might not realize it any more than she'd realized he was courting her, but she could have her pick.

"You think I should do something else?" he asked, pounding one of the shakes into place.

"Don't get your hopes up."

Harry peered down over the edge. "That bad?"

Jesse jiggled a plank to align it better. "No. You court good, Harry. I just don't want to see you all sad and mopey again."

Harry jerked back. "I don't mope."

"You do."

He sighed. "Maybe I do. For a time. Any man might be a little disappointed to have lost."

"That many times?"

Harry rolled his eyes. "Maybe it just took a while to find the right one."

"And you're sure Katie Jo is the right one?"

Said that way, doubts crept closer, like a mouse hunting for crumbs. She'd been under his nose, for months, and he hadn't paid her much mind. Was he acting more out of habit than hope?

Jesse banged another two planks into place before Harry found an answer he could live with. "I'm getting tired of playing the game, Jesse. I just want a wife, a family, a home. Is that too much to ask?"

For a moment, he was afraid his friend would tell him it was. Maybe Harry wasn't meant to have a family of his own. Maybe he hadn't earned it somehow.

"Nope," Jesse said. "You'd make a good husband and father. Keep trying."

Breath came easier. "I will."

They worked in a silence broken only by the bang of the hammer and the thump of the mallet.

"Thought you wanted the schoolmarm, though," Jesse said.

Harry hesitated. "The schoolmarm isn't here."

"Katie Jo deserves to be courted for more than being *here*."

Harry grimaced. "I'm not courting her because she's available, Jesse. I'm courting her because she's sweet and pretty."

"And available."

"Well, if she wasn't available, no one could court her, could they?" He pounded a shake so hard it split. He pried the pieces up and tossed them out into the yard.

"All I'm saying is that a gal wants to be wanted for herself, not for how she'll look on a fellow's arm," Jesse said. "Leastwise, that's what my ma and sisters tell me."

Jesse was the oldest of ten, and four of his siblings were sisters. He had more experience dealing with females of various ages and families in general than Harry would ever have. Harry grunted and set the last shake into place.

Jesse's big hands appeared on the edge of the porch roof as he lifted himself up to meet Harry's gaze. "So, are you going to court the schoolmarm too?"

He shouldn't. He'd never appreciated it when gals played one suitor off against the other. He wasn't about to do that to Katie Jo.

But what if the schoolteacher was as pretty and sweet as Katie Jo, but educated and cultured to boot? Hadn't he learned prudence from his previous courtships? Wouldn't it be better for his future children if he looked before he leaped?

Something in him recoiled, like he'd shot a round at a buck for the first time. "I'm not planning to switch paddles in the middle of a stream," he told Jesse. "Still, I suppose it would be best for me and Katie Jo that we're both sure of the matter."

Jesse disappeared below the edge of the roof. "Remember that, Harry. You aren't the only one who has to be sure about marrying. No matter who you end up choosing."

Katie Jo was changing the bedding in the chicken coop on Wednesday, tossing out the damp fir shavings to be dried and burned in the yard and replacing them with clean shavings, when she spotted movement among the cedars. They hadn't had any strangers up this way recently, so she'd taken to leaving her shotgun in the house. Now, the best she could do was pull up the pail full of shavings and hold it ready to hurl at any danger.

But instead of danger, Harry walked out of the woods with Ciara at his side. Both were dressed in their nicer clothes, as if they were out for a stroll after services. The pail plopped onto the ground from fingers gone numb.

She let herself out the gate in the chicken run and latched it behind her to a chorus of concerned clucks, then hurried to meet them. "Ciara, Harry, what's wrong?"

"Must something be wrong to come visit a friend?" Ciara asked with a smile. Marriage seemed to suit her, for her cheeks were a pretty pink, and her dark eyes sparkled.

"Well," Katie Jo hedged, "you never came to visit before."

"I didn't have time to visit before," Ciara told her. "And I don't have much now, especially if I can't convince you to keep working for me." She glanced at her escort. "Harry tells me you might be thinking of quitting."

Katie Jo looked to the house in time to catch sight of a shadow behind the slats on the front window. Likely Zeke was wondering what was keeping her. Thank goodness Uncle Cole was out checking his traps and wouldn't be listening in on this conversation.

"How's your brother?" Harry asked, as if he'd noticed her look.

"Better," Katie Jo told him. "And that's one of the reasons I'm thinking of quitting, Ciara. Zeke sickens pretty much every time I'm gone."

Her friend craned her neck as if trying to spy the lad as well. "I still don't understand why you can't bring him with you."

Maybe it would be best if she showed Ciara. "Come inside and meet him."

She hurried to the door, but before she could open it, Harry reached around her and opened it for her. She'd seen other gents do that for ladies as a courtesy, but the fact that Harry had done it for her made her flannels feel even warmer.

"Company, Zeke!" she called as she entered. Then she turned to Ciara and Harry. "Please, have a seat. I always keep a pot of coffee ready. Would you like some?"

"That would be lovely," Ciara said, going to seat herself on one of the rockers.

She probably hadn't noticed the shadow clinging to one corner of the room, but Katie Jo had. "Come and meet our guests, Zeke," she said, pitching her voice to carry. "This is Mrs. Weatherly, the proprietress of the Wooden Rose Inn. You remember Mr. Yeager."

Her brother eased out of the darkness. He must have threaded his fingers through his hair, because it was lying down more than usual, and his suspenders were properly up over his shoulders. He nodded to Ciara and Harry. "Ma'am. Mr. Yeager."

"Call me Harry," Harry said, taking one of the chairs by the table and turning it to face Ciara and Zeke before seating himself. Katie Jo knew she should not take such pleasure in the fact that he looked so well in her home.

Ciara shot Zeke a wide smile. "Mr. McAllister, it's a pleasure to meet you. Your sister has told me so much about you."

Zeke glanced to Katie Jo. "You did?"

"All good," Katie Jo assured him, making sure he could see her lips. "Will you put some of those cookies we baked on a plate for our guests? I'll get Ma's teacups."

His eyes widened, and he hurried for the table. He knew she only allowed him and their uncle to use the china with its pretty yellow roses on birthdays, Christmas, and Easter. "Coming right up."

She ducked behind her curtain to open her mother's chest and draw out two of the precious cups and saucers. Zeke had cried for days after breaking one couple of the set, so they only had seven now. But serving her friends, especially Harry, was worth the risk of losing another.

"How was the honeymoon?" she asked as she carried the cups and saucers to the table and set them down beside Harry. His brows went up as if he were impressed with them. Zeke offered him a plate of cookies. Katie Jo tried not to watch him eat it.

"The honeymoon was lovely," Ciara said, leaning back in the rocker with a contented sigh. "We stayed at the Occidental Hotel. No work, no estate business, just me and Kit." She eyed Katie Jo as she grabbed a towel and came to fetch the coffee pot from where it nestled next to the grate. "The restaurant served a fish stew with a tomato base. I'm itching to try it."

Zeke popped up on her other side and thrust the tin plate at her. "Cookie?"

"Why, thank you, Mr. McAllister." She selected one and took a bite.

This time, Katie Jo did pause to watch. So did her brother.

Ciara cocked her head. "Is that… anise?"

She grinned. "Mr. James Wallin traded me some aniseed for eggs. Finally had a chance to try it. Zeke likes it."

"So do I," Harry said, half-eaten cookie in one hand.

That smile! Why, she might have thought she'd swum all the way across Puget Sound to be met at Port Gamble by a brass band. She nearly forgot what she was about, until the warmth under her fingers reminded her.

She carried the pot to the table and poured the black

brew into the cups. "Well, I watched Ciara bake enough that I had to try something on my own. Anyone want sugar for the coffee?"

"You're sweet enough for me," Harry said with a wink.

"None for me either," Ciara said with an amused shake of her head at Harry.

Katie Jo forced her hands to remain steady as she carried a cup first to Ciara and then Harry. Zeke was making the rounds with the cookie plate again.

"You know," Ciara said after taking a sip of the coffee, "I'd like you to teach me how you made those cookies. We can add them to the rotation."

The honor of it raised her head. Her cooking, on Ciara's menu! "Thank you. I'd be glad to show you."

"Maybe I could come too," Zeke said, sinking down onto the chair next to Harry's.

"You would be welcome," Ciara assured him.

Zeke grinned at Katie Jo.

She grinned back. "Now we just need to convince Uncle Cole to allow it."

"That will take some convincing," her uncle said, coming through the rear door.

Katie Jo nearly slumped, despite her corset. Uncle Cole never liked surprises. She'd have little chance of persuading him now.

Zeke had his back to the door and obviously hadn't heard their uncle come in. "What about Friday?" he asked Ciara.

"Nonsense." Uncle Cole reached Katie Jo's side and nodded to Harry and Ciara before turning to Zeke and raising his voice. "You. Stay. Here." He pointed at the floor.

Zeke bristled, and Katie Jo set the coffee pot down on the table with a thud. Still, she kept her smile in place, conscious of her audience.

"Zeke's a little hard of hearing," she explained to Ciara

and Harry. "You just have to make sure he can see your lips, and he'll know what you're saying."

"If you're lucky," her uncle scoffed. He looked to Harry. "I see you already found another gal to court. Coming to let her gloat?"

Ciara colored.

"I think there's been a misunderstanding," Harry said smoothly as he stood from the table. "This is Mrs. Weatherly, who runs the Wooden Rose Inn at Wallin Landing. She wanted to talk to Katie Jo about her work. I was available to escort her." He grinned at Katie Jo. "And I'd take any excuse to come calling."

The room brightened, and birds sang outside, and she wouldn't have been surprised if the chickens had joined in.

"Are you having a problem with the girl?" her uncle asked Ciara. "She usually gives me a good day's work, more than most men I could name."

Ciara's face tightened. "Katie Jo is only a blessing. I've never seen anyone work so hard and so well. I heard she might be reconsidering working for me, so I thought I would come speak to her directly."

Katie Jo watched her uncle. Those green eyes flickered, as if thoughts ran like a river, fast and deep, behind them. He wiggled his lips a moment, setting his beard to wiggling too.

"She might be available," he mused, "for a price."

CHAPTER NINE

O H, NO. KATIE Jo was not about to let her uncle swindle her friends.

"Never mind him," she told Ciara. "You pay me plenty."

"You never did know your own worth, girl," her uncle said with a shake of his head. "Let me negotiate for you."

She wasn't the only one who questioned her worth, but in this, she would not be gainsaid.

"I'm of age," she said, raising her chin, "and it's my job. I can negotiate if it suits me."

Zeke grabbed her hand and gave it a tug, gaze pleading. He knew who would get the licking if she protested overly much.

"No need to negotiate," Harry put in. His smile was still in place too, but there was a tension in him now, like a bowstring drawn taut. "Mrs. Weatherly will be glad to pay whatever you feel is warranted."

Ciara shot him a frown, but said nothing.

"Dollar a day," her uncle said. "In silver."

"She only pays me two bits a day!" Katie Jo protested. "You're asking her to double my salary, for nothing."

"Done," Harry said. "We'll expect you Friday afternoon, Katie Jo." He nodded to her. "Ma'am. Zeke. Mr. McAllister."

Ciara looked like she was ready to mutiny, eyes snapping

fire and mouth a thin line, but she rose from the rocker and gave Katie Jo's uncle a curt nod before glancing at her. "I'll see you on Friday, Katie Jo. And Zeke, you're welcome too."

"That will be another dollar a day," Uncle Cole said.

Ciara puffed up like a hen prepared to battle a snake who was out to steal her eggs. Harry took her hand and escorted her out.

As soon as the door had shut behind them, Uncle Cole rounded on Katie Jo. "Don't you ever contradict me in front of others again, girl."

"Then don't you go ordering my life," she snapped back. "Those are my friends."

"Some friends, who wrangle over pay. Be glad I got you a raise." He started for the washtub.

Katie Jo tailed him. "I didn't ask for a raise because I didn't need one. She pays me fine."

He stopped and scowled at her. "Fine? Did you see how she was dressed? She has a whole inn, while we barely make ends meet. Folks like us have to stand up to those who try to take advantage of us."

"Seems I do," Katie Jo said.

He missed the sarcasm. "That's why I'm here. You and Zeke need me. It's my job to protect you. Now, come out to the crick. There's someone I want you to meet."

She didn't want to go anywhere with him, but he'd likely take any further protests out on Zeke, so she nodded.

"Be careful," Zeke murmured as she followed her uncle out the rear door.

Across the creek from the cabin, a man waited. Like some who lived in the woods, he was dressed in buckskin trousers and a gingham shirt. His grizzled hair hung down in limp locks on either side of a face as tanned as leather. Sharp gray eyes regarded her as she approached the bank.

"This your niece?" he asked in a gravelly voice.

"Katie Jo," her uncle said, "meet Martin Delany."

Katie Jo nodded. "Mr. Delany."

He looked her up and down again, then spit tobacco into the creek. "I'm looking for a gal, but I heard you was set to marry."

Heat flushed up her. "No, sir. I don't reckon too many fellows would cotton to me."

He ran his gaze over her again. "Maybe. Maybe more than you think."

She felt as if he'd spit the tobacco on her instead of into the water. "Well, it makes no never mind. I didn't figure on marrying."

"Until recently," her uncle put in. "Fellow down from Wallin Landing way has been sniffing around. He was in the house just now. I scared him off."

That's what he thought. He'd never seen Harry courting. Like a dog to a bone that one.

"Harry Yeager doesn't scare so easily," Katie Jo told him.

Her uncle chuckled. "Oh, you might be surprised. I should check on your brother. Fool's like as not to burn himself in the fire if you don't watch him every minute. You just have a nice conversation with Marty." He nodded to his friend and headed for the house.

"You like salmon?" Marty asked.

She frowned at him. "Sure. Most folks like salmon."

He nodded. "I'll bring you some. You sew?"

"Well enough to put a button back on and mend a tear," she allowed. "Not the fancy stuff like Mrs. Wallin down at the Landing."

He nodded again. "What about cooking?"

Was he interviewing her for a job? Ciara hadn't asked half so many questions! "I can skin a rabbit and turn it into a nice stew. I can dress a deer and dry venison."

He edged closer to his side of the creek, sucking a tooth. "And baking? Can you do that?"

She was learning from Ciara. "Some. I can make anise cookies and spotted pup."

"What's spotted pup?" he asked with a frown.

"Rice pudding with raisins and cinnamon."

His smile turned up. "That sounds good." He glanced at the house. "Not too picky on where you sleep either, I bet."

"Picky enough," Katie Jo said, heat rising with her temper. "Now, I should get back to my chores. I'm sure you and my uncle have plenty to talk about. I'll leave you to it."

She backed toward the house and didn't take her eyes off him until she'd slipped through the rear doorway, where she found her uncle watching.

"He has possibilities," he said.

At least he'd tried to play chaperone. Zeke might have served, but he'd crawled back into bed and pulled the covers up over his ears, his way of screening out the world.

"What kind of possibilities?" Katie Jo asked, going to wash her hands in the basin, anything to remove the feeling that she'd plunged them in chicken droppings. "You already insisted on a raise for me. I don't want to work for him too."

He barked a laugh. "Marty isn't here about a job, girl. He's thinking about courting."

She shook the water from her hands. "Not with me, he isn't."

Her uncle shrugged. "I know you have your heart set on that Yeager fellow. All I'm doing is seeing if there's other interest out there." He moved closer and met her gaze. "It never hurts to have choices. You'll see."

"That," Ciara said as Harry turned with her onto the path south along the lake, "was uncalled for."

Harry couldn't argue. The way Katie Jo's uncle talked to her and Zeke made him boil faster than a pot over a hot fire. So what if the boy was hard of hearing? That didn't mean anything else was difficult for him. And Cole McAllister ought to be encouraging Katie Jo, not implying she was helpless without him.

"You had no right to agree to a raise," Ciara continued, brushing aside a branch that snapped back and struck him mid-chest. "It's my restaurant, and anything Katie Jo has to say, she can say to me."

"I know," Harry said, edging around her to help her up over a tree that had fallen onto the path. "And she was trying to say it. Her uncle just didn't want to listen."

"Well," Ciara huffed, "you got that right."

"With all the folks coming to eat you can't afford a dollar a day?" he asked as the waters of the lake winked at them through the firs.

"Not yet," Ciara said. "Between the cost of the food and the supplies needed to fix the upstairs, we're barely keeping solvent. As it is, I may have to hire a carpenter if Drew keeps needing Kit so long each day."

"I'll help with the upstairs," Harry offered.

She slanted him a glance. "I thought you were busy working on your cabin."

"I am," he said. "But the cabin doesn't matter if the lady who'll be occupying it is living at the other end of Lake Union."

She shook her head. "So you *are* courting Katie Jo."

"I'm getting a little tired of folks doubting that," Harry said, shoving back a fern that waved too close. "Yes, I'm courting her. She's not making it easy."

"Good," Ciara said primly. Then she grinned at him. "Easily won is little valued. You remember that, Harry." Her smile faded. "Now I just have to find the money."

"Do what you can," Harry said. "I'll pay the difference."

"Oh, Harry, no!" Ciara cried. "That's too much."

"Not from where I stand," he said. "A dollar a day is an investment in my future. And she's worth it."

Her smile softened. "You really are a romantic."

Harry jerked to a stop and stared at her as she picked her way past on the muddy trail, skirts held high with one hand. "A *romantic!*"

"Yes," Ciara said over her shoulder. "A man who appreciates the romance in life, even if he refuses to admit it!"

If that wasn't enough to set a fellow back, he didn't know what was. Him, a romantic. He'd always thought himself a realist, knowing the dark that backed the light. He appreciated the joys of life and dealt with the unpleasant matters as they came. He wasn't looking for a wife for the romance so much as a partner, a family. Any romantic notions, or actions, were only to get the gal's attention.

He was still mulling over the matter when they came into the Landing to find a crowd gathered in front of the inn.

"Oh, now what?" Ciara asked.

They hurried forward. At least a dozen men were clustered around, jostling each other as if trying to get a look at something in the middle. He recognized the blacksmith at the edge.

Jesse's head stuck up above the others. He had his arms high, ready to help a woman down from what was likely the buckboard. She had hair thick, dark, and curling down behind her, and fine features, like a countess he'd seen once in a painting at one of the fancy Seattle hotels. He couldn't see much of her figure or her dress except from her shoulders to her waist, but everything appeared dainty and fragile.

"I'll carry your bag for you, ma'am," one of the prospectors offered.

"I'll carry your trunk," one of the other loggers in the area insisted.

"Let me open the door for you," a young farmer begged, going so far as to jump onto the porch of the inn.

"Thank you, gentlemen," she said in a soft voice that reminded Harry of the notes of a flute. She paused before allowing Jesse to hand her down. "Everyone has been so kind. But I believe there are accommodations at the school for me. At least, that was what I was promised."

It seemed the new schoolmarm had arrived in Wallin Landing at last.

In the end, Uncle Cole allowed Katie Jo to bring Zeke with her when she went in to the Landing on Friday. It took some talking. But her arguments that she needed to fetch the mail and Zeke would be out of his hair for two days seemed to have done the trick. Still, she felt him watching them all the way through the cedars.

"He ain't never going to let us go," Zeke said as they trudged toward the lake. His steps didn't falter, and she liked to think he had a little more color than when she'd first come home from the wedding.

"He will," Katie Jo said, hitching up her pack on her shoulder. "And you remember what Mrs. Wallin taught us at the school years ago. Ain't ain't a word. You have to talk better than that at the Landing if you want folks to respect you."

He wrinkled his nose. "I don't recall them respecting us much before."

She raised her chin. "We were children then. Now, we're grown."

He stuck his thumbs in his suspenders. "I like that. I'm a man grown. Just you remember that too."

"Let's not get carried away," she said with a wink.

Zeke laughed.

Her heart flipped in her chest. This was what her brother needed—encouragement, a chance to get away from the house and the claim. An opportunity to try new things.

Still, she couldn't help worrying a little as they turned south along the lake and onto the longer leg of the trip. Was this going to be too much for him? He didn't seem to be limping. Indeed, his gaze darted here, there, everywhere, as if he wanted to hug everything close. She knew the feeling. It seemed the whole world opened up once they left the claim.

"We could stay at the inn, if it isn't finished yet," she told her brother as they clambered over a fallen log. "But if they finished sooner than expected, we might have to make other arrangements."

"I don't mind," he said, slipping down the other side. "So long as it don't... doesn't rain."

She glanced up at the clouds, speared on the tips of the firs. "Sky's mighty low. But I don't think they'll put us outside. I hear there's a room off the school, for the teacher. Mrs. Wallin doesn't need it, so we might be able to stay there."

He cast her another glance. "You're not taking me back to school."

The other children hadn't been particularly kind to her brother. Rina Wallin had been good about standing where he could read her lips and helping him quietly, so as not to single him out. But some of the younger boys had called him names and made faces at him when they were in the yard in front of the school.

"You're too old for school now," Katie Jo said. "Still, it never hurts to keep learning. I wouldn't have this job if I hadn't been willing to learn how to help Ciara, Mrs. Weatherly."

"I'd like to learn a trade," he mused, ducking under a

low-hanging branch on his side of the path. "Blacksmith, maybe, or logger, like Harry."

She looked at her brother's spindly arms and didn't have the heart to tell him he'd never be able to wield a hammer or an axe to do either job. "I always liked helping Mr. Wallin at the mercantile. You never know what sorts of goods or people might show up."

Her brother nodded, as if giving the matter thought, and she let it go at that.

But her mind kept tumbling the matter over, like pebbles in the waves. What was to become of her brother? Even if she convinced Uncle Cole to let them move into Wallin Landing permanently, someone would have to look out for him. She couldn't leave him alone for hours while she worked, and she doubted even Ciara would want him underfoot every day.

"Almost there!" he sang out as they passed the first cabin, the one Harry and Jesse were sharing now. The steeply roofed log structure had been Simon Wallin's, then Beth's, then Ciara's. Maybe it would be empty when Jesse finished his cabin, and she and her brother could stay there.

"Come on," Zeke urged, moving faster. "I want to see the inn."

So did she, but for another reason entirely. It was getting late in the afternoon, and sometimes Drew Wallin let his crew off early on Friday. Maybe Harry would be waiting.

The trees parted, and there was the village center. Already, men were lined up on the porch of the inn, waiting for Ciara to turn the sign to Open and signal that dinner was ready. In the far field, Lancelot and Percival were cropping the grass, with the milk cow, which had been a present from the Wallin family to Ciara and Kit for their wedding, shuffling about nearby. Their chicken run near the barn was neat and tidy, the hens pecking contently. And children were playing on the big swings hanging from the cedars near the school, their voices sharp in the fall air.

"Don't remember those," Zeke mused beside her. He was walking a little closer now, as if hugging her warmth.

"Kit Weatherly built them," she offered, t rying t o keep her gaze from darting around like her brother's. It wouldn't do her any good to have Harry know how much she'd missed him. "You could try one. They're big enough to hold your weight."

He snorted. "Men don't sit on swings." Still, his gaze lingered.

Hers had stopped on the door to the school. A lady she didn't recognize had come out to wish the last children farewell for the day. Her hair was as shiny as a jet bead, and everything from her fine-boned face to her fi gure was dainty.

"Is that the new schoolmarm?" Zeke whispered, as if afraid she might fly off the stoop and capture him if he spoke louder.

"Must be," Katie Jo said, aware of the same lowering of her spirits she'd felt when she'd first seen herself in a dress without the corset.

Miss Dennison stepped to one side and spoke to someone still in the school. A moment later, and Harry climbed down onto the ground. She put a hand on his shoulder and smiled sweetly at him. The look twisted like a branch stuck in Katie Jo's chest.

"I should have known," she murmured.

Zeke frowned. "Why's Harry being so nice to her?"

She put her back to them and started for the inn. "Harry's always nice to every pretty girl that comes out this way."

"But he's courting you," Zeke protested, scurrying to keep up.

She slowed her steps. "Harry Yeager has better things to do than hang after me."

Zeke's face turned mulish. "That's not fair."

"Life ain't fair," she said. "But that doesn't mean we shouldn't keep trying." She pushed past the prospectors, farmers, and loggers crowding the door. "One side, gents. You don't eat until I set the tables for you."

"Then right this way," the first said, pulling off his hat and bumping into the others to nudge them aside. "Wouldn't want to keep a feller from doing his duty."

CHAPTER TEN

ALICE DENNISON WAS pretty as a picture. She was smarter than Harry too, he had no doubt, yet she didn't make him feel as if she realized that. But Harry had gone from admiring her delicate looks to marveling that she was so helpless. A fellow didn't mind being the strong one and assisting his lady when needed. But Miss Dennison didn't even know how to start a fire to warm up the school or gather eggs like one of the youngest Wallin daughters.

"It was very kind of you, Mr. Yeager, to show me how to lay the wood properly in the grate," she said now in her soft voice. "I should be able to handle it tomorrow."

At least she was a fast learner. She just had so much to learn. Her white, frilly dress made him think of one of Maddie Haggerty's fancy cakes, but one day in the classroom with her grubby-handed children and already it was sagging and stained. Her hair might look like spun silk, but it was curling out of its confinement to tickle her perfect cheeks. And he knew all too well how those purple-blue eyes could tear up and tear into a man's heart.

"You'll be fine," he said. "You need anything else this afternoon, you ask Mr. Willets."

She peered past him toward the path to their cabin. "Mr. Willets seems to have taken me in dislike."

Jesse Willets was terrified, more like. At the first sign of her cultured ways and fine talk, he'd high-tailed it to their cabin and shut himself in. Of the unmarried men in the area, only that lawyer, Dixon Hitchcock, seemed to know what to make of her. He'd showed up last night with yet more papers for Kit to sign.

"A lady through and through," he'd told Harry. "I'm surprised she agreed to come West."

So was Harry. Miss Dennison seemed destined for fancy parlors, fine china, and fussy committee meetings with other ladies too proper to do anything else. He had never intended to marry a gal who couldn't be comfortable in his world. Katie Jo suited him just fine.

The thought of her hastened his steps across the clearing. When he'd come through earlier, the line had begun forming for the Wooden Rose. Now it stretched all the way down the boardwalk in front, and a couple bold fellows were up on the rear porch and peering through the window by the door. Harry whistled sharply, which made their heads come up, then jerked his thumb toward the line. They slumped and shambled back into place.

"Haven't they heard that Ciara O'Rourke is now Ciara Weatherly?" he asked Old Joe, who was near the front of the line.

"Not Mrs. Weatherly they came to see," he said. "That new gal is helping her. Seems Mrs. Weatherly fired that young feller who was here afore."

She'd fired Katie Jo? That's the only young fellow he could mean. She'd been so much in the kitchen or the background that some must not have realized she was a girl. But surely Ciara wouldn't fire her best worker, not after she'd reluctantly agreed to a raise.

To shouts of protest, Harry shoved past the men and pushed open the door, shutting it firmly behind him when a couple tried to follow him in. All the tables were in place, and most were set with cutlery and napkins. Katie Jo was standing by the big table that had once held the Wallin family, Zeke at her side. She wore a blue gingham dress, fitted at the waist and emphasizing her curves, and her hair was falling down behind her like a dollop of honey from a spoon.

"It's real easy," she was saying with a nod toward the place settings. "You just pick up the plates, forks, and knives when they're done with them and bring them to me to wash. Then you take some of the clean ones and set the table for the next batch of customers."

Her brother nodded, blond hair tipping over his forehead.

"Your sister makes it look easy," Harry said, approaching them. "But I bet it's harder than we think."

Her head came up, and she met his gaze, only to look away, color climbing in her cheeks. "You better get your dinner now and take it back to your cabin, Harry. We got a line outside."

"I saw it," he said. "But I wasn't planning on leaving my best gal alone with that mob."

She edged away from him. "I'm sure Ciara will be glad to hear that. She can always use another pair of hands." She hurried for the kitchen.

Her brother stayed where he was, glaring at Harry. "Maybe your new lady would like dinner too. You should take it to her."

Harry frowned at him. "What are you talking about?"

He tipped his head toward the window. "The new schoolmarm. You looked real comfortable together."

Harry blinked. "I was helping Miss Dennison with the fire. Drew asked me."

Zeke snorted. "Nice excuse."

Harry took a step closer. "I don't know where you got the idea I'm not constant. When I set out to court a gal,

I court her until she tells me she'd prefer otherwise. I haven't heard your sister say that."

He raised his chin. "She will. She has all those fellers out there to choose from now. And Uncle Cole says Mr. Delaney from up our way is planning on courting her too."

The savory scents of Ciara's pork and apple pie turned to ash. "Then it sounds like I better get a move on. Thanks for the warning."

He frowned at Harry. "You mean that? You really are set on Katie Jo?"

"With all my heart," Harry said, laying a hand on his chest. "You watch the next two days, and you'll see."

Katie Jo hadn't intended to wear her other dress for work. She'd originally commissioned it from Nora before the wedding to wear for church, and she didn't want to get it dirty. Even with one of Ciara's shoulder-to-hem canvas aprons covering her, she was sure to slop water or food on a sleeve.

But after seeing Miss Dennison in her prim and frilly glory, she just had to give it a try. She might not have time to heat a curling iron, if Ciara even had one, but she could tame her hair back from her face.

She wasn't disappointed in the reactions.

"Let me carry one of those for you, missy," Old Joe said when she came out of the kitchen with a plate on each hand. "Pretty little thing like you shouldn't have to work so hard."

"If I was your husband," one of the ranchers put in, leaning back in his chair to eye her up and down, "you wouldn't have to lift one dainty little foot."

Her? Dainty? She nearly snorted, then remembered she was supposed to be acting like a lady. "Thank you, sir," she said to Old Joe as she set the plate down in front of the rancher. "But I don't bruise so easily."

"I bet she don't," someone said. She thought he sounded admiring.

"I can help you wash up," one of the other loggers in the area offered, laying down a fat consideration beside his plate. "Bet we could be real cozy working together at that sink."

Too cozy. "I need to earn my keep," she told him, taking his plate. "But if you want to help, you could go chop us some wood."

"On my way," he said, rising and heading for the door.

"Don't encourage them," Ciara said as Katie Jo returned to the kitchen. "Dottie told me the way a logger says he loves you is by chopping wood for you. Jesse and Harry nearly filled the front room before I could dissuade them."

Katie Jo glanced out at the pile beside the big stone hearth. It didn't look all that high to her. And she hadn't seen hide nor hair of Harry since dinner had started.

As if the mere thought had cut him out of whole cloth, he came in, arms full of wood. She ducked out of sight and stared at Ciara.

"What's wrong?" Ciara asked, bending to pull the last pie out of the oven.

"Harry just came in with wood," she whispered.

Ciara grinned. "Told you."

"Maybe it's just extra from what he chopped for the schoolteacher," she hedged, rolling up her sleeves to keep them out of the dishwater. Why had Nora made them so tight? She hardly had room to turn them.

"Jesse's been keeping the schoolhouse well supplied," Ciara said, cutting the pie into eight slices with quick efficiency.

"Bet Harry doesn't like that." She plunged her arms into the soapy water and began scrubbing at a plate.

"Harry doesn't seem to care," Ciara said. "I think he has another lady in mind."

Katie Jo's head rocked back on her neck. "Oh, not another one!"

"No, silly!" Ciara came over to nudge her with her shoulder. "You!"

She shook her head, but her hair began to slip. So she toweled off her hands, stepped aside, and put it back in place, then had to wash her hands again before carrying out the next set of plates.

Harry sent her a smile that made her stomach feel like it was a salmon leaping out of the bay for pure joy. But before she could decide whether she was willing to acknowledge him, he ducked out the door again. Shaking her head, she returned to the kitchen.

Zeke had been outside sweeping off the rear porch as a favor to Ciara. He came in now, dusting off his hands. Two spots of color stood high on his cheeks, but his smile was game.

"You tired?" Katie Jo asked, heading back to the sink.

"Nope," Zeke said, joining her. "There's too much to see. Did you know Mrs. Nora has a three-legged cow?"

"I've seen it," she said. "She's real sweet. What were you doing up on the farm?"

"Talking with Mr. Wallin, her husband. Thought he might be able to use a hand on his farm, for when we move in."

The idea of her brother out behind a set of oxen plowing the field was as bad as him trying to take up blacksmithing or logging. "What did he say?"

"Said he wouldn't know for certain until spring, but he was hopeful. Tomorrow, I'll ask Mr. Wallin at the mercantile." He took a dish she had just washed and began drying it. "Sure are a lot of Mr. Wallins around here."

"Mrs. Wallins too," Katie Jo agreed.

"Plates ready," Ciara called, and Katie Jo turned to help with the next batch.

"Wouldn't you like to join me, Miss McAllister?" the rancher said as she laid down his pie. "There's room at the table, and I could buy you a plate."

"I'm working, not eating," she reminded him.

"Maybe another time?" he wheedled, brows up as if in hope.

"She's always working," Zeke said, passing with a plate for another table.

He frowned after the boy.

"That's my brother," Katie Jo said. "He's a mite protective."

"I would be too if I had a sister like you," he said with a nod, frown easing.

The door opened, but no one came in. Had the wind caught it? She hadn't noticed a storm brewing. Katie Jo hurried to shut it.

Before she could, Miss Dennison minced into the room, two fellows bowing and scraping after her. Her gaze lit on Katie Jo, and her smile turned up. Those birds must be singing in the woods again.

"I just came for a plate," she said in a voice Katie Jo thought the singers in the touring companies must envy. "Whatever's easy."

At least she didn't demand the best and in a hurry. Katie Jo couldn't help but like that.

"We got vegetable soup and a pork and apple pie tonight," she said. "Plenty of both left. Which would you prefer?"

"You can eat with me, miss," the rancher who'd just been ogling Katie Jo offered, sliding his chair over. "Young McAllister could fetch you a chair."

"Busy," Zeke said, brushing past.

"No, thank you," Miss Dennison said. "I have a lesson to prepare for Monday."

"Don't see why you couldn't prepare it here, beside me," another called.

Others chorused their eagerness to have her join them.

"That's enough," Katie Jo said, and the voices snapped off like she'd shut the door on the church choir. "Can't a lady get a moment of peace without you lot jabbering at her?"

Grumbling, they went back to their dinners.

"Thank you," the schoolteacher said, following Katie Jo to the kitchen. "I never dreamed walking through the door could cause such a clamor."

"You just have to stand up to them," Katie Jo said.

"Good evening, Ciara," Miss Dennison said with a nod to the cook.

"How are you fairing, Alice?" Ciara asked.

So, they were already using first names. It had taken Katie Jo a while to accustom herself to it. It seemed intimate, somehow, like they knew her better than she knew herself.

"I'm gradually settling in," Miss Dennison said with a humble smile. "It's just so different from where I was raised."

"Miss Dennison is from the Boston area," Ciara explained, adding a slice of her Irish barmbrack bread to the plate. "She attended the same teacher's college as Rina."

"Long way to come to teach," Katie Jo said, bringing Ciara a clean bowl for the soup.

"I was looking for a fresh start," Miss Dennison replied. "My, but that pie looks good, Ciara."

"I'll fix you up a plate right now," Ciara said.

"I can do it," Katie Jo offered, grabbing a plate. "You two probably want to talk."

Miss Dennison's laugh was like sunlight on a meadow. "I learned right away it wasn't wise to interrupt the chef at her work."

Ciara laughed as well. "Chef. I like that. But I like proprietress better. A few more nights of work from Harry and the others, and we'll have this inn ready for customers. Then I can open six nights a week. That is, if I can convince someone to stay at Wallin Landing."

"You don't have to convince me," Katie Jo said, setting the pie on the plate and following it with some honeyed carrots. "You just need to help me convince Uncle Cole."

"Katie Jo's uncle wants her to stay safely on the claim," Ciara explained for the schoolteacher's benefit.

"He wants Katie Jo to do all the work, more like," Zeke said, bustling back through to bring in some dirty dishes. "He's too lazy to do it himself."

"Zeke!" Katie Jo protested. "You know what he gave up for us."

"I do," Zeke said. "And I see what you're giving up too."

He hurried back out.

"I'm not giving up anything," Katie Jo assured Ciara, who was frowning. "I know my duty."

"It's not my place to say," Miss Dennison put in as Katie Jo handed her her plate, "but I'm learning that a lady's primary duty is to see to herself. Only then can she see to the needs of others."

Something about that didn't set right, but Katie Jo wasn't sure how to argue against it. Then, from out in the main room, another sound rose, a plunk, a squeak. She couldn't place it at first, especially under the rumble of male voices from the other diners. She angled her head to try to see what was happening.

Zeke barreled in again. "I swept under the big table. Four more just sat down."

Now another voice rose, even as the rumble faded.

"Who's that singing?" Miss Dennison asked.

Katie Jo knew. Singing or talking or whispering, she

was sure she'd know. It was Harry, and he was playing his
guitar.

"Oh, tell me that you love me yet
For, oh! The parting gives me pain.
Say, tell me that you'll not forget
For we may never meet again."
She sucked in a breath. Was he telling her this was
goodbye?

"We parted by the riverside
A teardrop trembled on your cheek.
In vain to tell my love I tried
My heart was sad. I could not speak.
I promised that I would be true
So long as I would live.
The parting kiss I gave to you
Was all I had to give."

As he launched into the chorus again, some began
hooting and hollering. Other voices shushed them. Ciara
wiped her hands on her apron, smile hovering. Katie Jo
couldn't seem to move.

"We parted by the riverside
And I have roamed a distant clime.
My heart has not forgot its pride,
For I have loved you all the time.
And I am faithful to you still,
While I believe you true.
Afar or near let come what will.
I'll love you, only you."
She stared at Ciara. "What do I do?"

Miss Dennison was smiling, misty-eyed. "If it were me,
I'd tell him I felt the same way." She blinked as if suddenly
realizing she might have overstepped. "That is, if you do
feel the same way."

"I don't know what I feel," Katie Jo said. "But I suppose
I should at least thank him for singing."

CHAPTER ELEVEN

HARRY IGNORED THE whistles and calls that shook the beams above him. He only cared what one listener thought. He kept his eyes on the door to the kitchen.

Katie Jo came out. She didn't look at him, taking two plates to a table near the hearth. The men thanked her kindly. She nodded and backed away.

Didn't she know that song was for her?

Gaze on her boots, sticking out below the hem of her gown, she wove her way through the other tables to his side.

"That was real nice, Harry," she said, studying the planks at his feet as if they held the answer to life itself. "Thank you."

"You're welcome," he said. "I hope you know I meant every word."

Her head came up, eyes wide and startled. "You did?"

He took her hand and cradled it in his. "Yes, darlin'. There's only one gal for me."

"That's cause there's only one unmarried gal in the whole area!" someone shouted, and the others laughed.

"Two if you count the schoolteacher," someone else put in.

"You really ought to let someone else give it a try,

Yeager," another hollered. "You can't keep all the pretty gals."

She was turning redder with each complaint.

"Maybe I should have waited until they were gone," he muttered.

She eyed him under her lashes. "I'm glad you didn't. It was beautiful."

He leaned closer. "No more beautiful than you."

She skuttled back so fast she nearly overset the closest table. "I best get back to work."

Harry shook his head as she vanished into the kitchen. He was still doing something wrong.

He took his guitar back to his cabin and returned to help clean up, but Ciara shooed him out.

"I have plenty of helpers tonight," she said. "Go to bed, Harry. I'll see you in the morning."

He leaned closer. "You wouldn't say that if it was you and Kit courting."

She put both hands on his shoulders and gave him a shove. "I didn't have to say that to Kit. Katie Jo needs time to think about things. Be a gentleman and give it to her."

He angled his head to try to see into the kitchen. Katie Jo and Zeke were both at the sink, one washing and the other drying.

"If she wants me gone," he told Ciara, "she can tell me."

Katie Jo turned to meet his gaze, her own shadowed. "Good night, Harry. See you in the morning."

Defeated, he inclined his head and left.

But he made sure to be one of the first in the door on Saturday.

"Katie Jo and Zeke are sleeping in this morning," Ciara said, plunking down a platter of griddle cakes. "I'm sure you'll see them when you get back from work."

Harry forked up two cakes and shook his head.

"Someone's in a dark mood," Kit said as they followed

Drew out into the forest a short time later. A cold mist hovered in the air, as if the clouds wanted to rest on the ground for a time, and everything was moist and musty smelling.

"You would be too if the woman you wanted to marry wouldn't give you the time of day," Harry grumbled, shifting his axe on his shoulder.

"She talks to you," Jesse pointed out from behind him.

"To be clear," Drew said, stopping in front of the last big fir they needed to cut down, "are we talking about Katie Jo McAllister or Alice Dennison?"

"Katie Jo McAllister!" Harry thundered, earning him a rare scowl from his boss.

Drew generally only worked a half day on Saturdays, so Harry hurried back as soon as the big woodsman gave the all clear. At least the clouds had risen up over the trees again, making everything more gray than wet. Maybe he could take Katie Jo for a walk, talk about their future.

But, once again, Ciara refused him entrance.

"We have work to do, Harry, and you'll only get in the way," she said, arms crossed over her chest as she stood in the front doorway.

Frustrated, he plopped down on the planks of the porch and prepared to wait until she turned the restaurant sign to Open.

Movement showed through the trees on the other side of the inn a moment before the blacksmith strode out of the path leading to the mercantile. His eight-year-old son was skipping along beside him, glancing up at his father from time to time as if completely content to be in such company. The smile his father bestowed on him said he felt the same way.

Harry couldn't remember his father looking at him that way. He couldn't remember his father much at all, truth be told. And none of the distant cousins had ever taken the time to walk with him, share a moment.

Cows need milking, boy. Hop to it.

Didn't I tell you to bring in more wood for the fire? What have you been doing all day?

If you weren't so worthless, maybe your ma and pa would have found a reason to live.

He pushed away the ugly memories. He was building his own family, one where encouragement and love would lead the way. He'd spend time with his children, help them grow up straight and strong, knowing their parents would always care.

Zeke, who had been hanging onto the rope supporting one of the big swings as if wondering whether to try sitting, crossed the space and dropped down beside him. "Busy place, ain't it?" Before Harry could answer, he grimaced. "Sorry. It's a busy place, don't you think?"

"I generally like busy," Harry said, glancing back over his shoulder at the door. Female voices echoed from within, punctuated by an occasional giggle. "Ciara said they were working. Does that sound like work to you?"

"They're planning another dress for Katie Jo," Zeke said with a sigh. "She already has two. Uncle Cole says trousers and shirts are more practical."

"More practical for us," Harry said. "There's something about a gal in a dress that makes a man look forward to the day."

Zeke frowned. "Why?"

"Ask me that in a couple years," Harry said with a grin. He rose. "Sounds like they're going to be busy for a while. I have work to do too."

Zeke sighed. "Wish I did."

Harry eyed him. "You want to help finish my cabin?"

"Would I!" The boy leapt to his feet. "Which way?"

Harry led him up through the woods to the claim. The boy stood a moment, glancing around with narrowed eyes, as if he saw more than the clearing and the trees surrounding it.

"Barn over there, I bet," he finally said.

Harry nodded. "That's right. How did you know?"

"Best drainage when it rains, and you're not too far from the creek to bring water." He frowned at the house. "I don't know why you didn't put boxes under the windows like at the inn. You could grow herbs right there to grab for dinner, and it would look nice too."

Harry considered the side of the cabin. "Good idea." He looked back at the boy. "How'd you get so smart?"

Zeke shrugged, though his lean cheeks were turning pink. "You lay around often enough, you have time to think about all sorts of things."

Harry nodded. "I bet you do. So maybe you can help me with something else."

"Sure," Zeke said eagerly.

"What can I do to please your sister?"

Katie Jo had thought Harry might poke his head in the door when the dining room opened at five, but she didn't catch sight of him until they'd fed the first ravenous round. Then he, Jesse, and Zeke showed up, begging plates. Ciara filled one for Jesse and Katie Jo's brother, but she tilted her head toward Harry.

"Why don't you serve him, Katie Jo?"

Ciara didn't fool her. She managed multiple plates all the time. She was matchmaking, plain and simple. Very likely that was why she'd brought Alice and Nora over that afternoon to talk about dresses.

Now Katie Jo pulled down one of the clean plates and slid in behind the big stove next to her friend. Ciara had told her that one of the reasons she'd known she might succeed in opening a restaurant in the settlement was this stove. Most folks in the area, like Katie Jo, cooked over the fire. Only a handful had any kind of stove, and nothing to match this black iron six-burner wonder with its two ovens, warming drawer, and silver trim. Now Katie Jo batted away the steam from the big kettle of soup with one hand and looked at Harry. "We have bean and bacon soup and beef stew tonight. Which would you prefer?"

He leaned against the door jamb. "Surprise me."

That steam was warmer than she'd expected, for her skin was heating. She slopped some stew on his plate and added two of Ciara's biscuits. No one quite matched those of Levi Wallin, but hers were the closest Katie Jo had ever tried.

"Much obliged," Harry said as he accepted the plate from her. "I'll be back for dessert."

He didn't even look at the blackcap pies on the sideboard.

She swallowed, watching out the door as he loped for the porch.

"You seen Miss Dennison?" Jesse asked, accepting his plate from Ciara.

"Not since this afternoon," she admitted. "And it's a full house at the moment, so I'm not sure where I'd put her if she did come looking."

He nodded. "Fill me another plate. I'll take it to her."

"That's real nice of you, Jesse," Katie Jo told him, grabbing up several of the biscuits to add to the plate Ciara was putting together.

"Just being neighborly," he said. He accepted the plate with a nod of thanks to them both and followed Harry out the door.

"Thanks," Zeke said, taking his plate from Ciara. "Don't suppose you have any of that lemon pound cake left from last night."

Ciara smiled at him. "I saved a slice just for you. It's down in the root cellar. If I left it up here, someone was bound to eat it."

He grinned, set his plate on the sideboard out of the way, then propped open the hatch that would let him down into the root cellar. Kit had recently installed the door, so Ciara didn't have to go outside every time she wanted access to the storage room.

Katie Jo glanced out the doorway in time to see more men enter the restaurant. "Two came in," she reported. "They're taking the table by the stairs, which just emptied. Best I get it cleaned fast."

From down in the root cellar came a thump and a cry. She froze.

Ciara must have heard the noises too, for she started forward. "I'll see to them. Check on Zeke."

With a nod, Katie Jo scrambled for the hatch.

A short ladder led down into the ground beneath the cabin. The Wallin father had excavated a space that ran under most of the kitchen and out onto the garden, where another door could be used to access it. Kit must have factored in Ciara's skirts when he'd designed the new opening, for Katie Jo had no trouble navigating the rungs in her dress. The light pouring down from the kitchen allowed her to make out a figure slumped among the sacks of cornmeal and flour.

"Zeke!" Keeping her head down, for the space wasn't tall enough for her to stand upright, she scurried over to her brother.

He sat up, rubbing his head. "Don't fuss. I'm fine."

"Are you?" Katie Jo peered closer. He looked as if he'd paled again, and she thought she detected a tremor in his fingers. She crouched and started running her hands over his legs. "What happened?"

"Talk louder," he said, pushing away her hands. "I can't see your lips down here."

"Sorry," she said, raising her voice as she rocked back on her heels. "What happened?"

"Bent to pick up a rock in the way, then straightened and hit my head." He scowled up at the beams crossing the ceiling and supporting the kitchen. "I guess I'm taller than I thought."

She stood carefully and offered him a hand to help him rise. "You're growing. Only to be expected."

He glanced around, spotted the wrapped piece of poundcake lying half open in the dirt, where he must have dropped it in his fall, then picked it up and sighed. "Well, I ruined this, I guess."

"There are ginger snaps for dessert tonight," Katie Jo told him, directing him toward the ladder. "A serving is two. You can have four."

She caught his grin before he climbed up ahead of her.

Ciara was back at the stove, stirring the soup. "Everything all right?" she asked.

"Everything's fine," Katie Jo assured her, shutting the hatch behind her. "Eat your dinner, Zeke, then you can commence sweeping."

"Yes, ma'am," he said before grabbing his plate and four of the cookies and heading out the back door.

"He's a good lad, your brother," Ciara said, ladling some of the soup into a bowl. "I don't understand why your uncle won't let him come in more often."

"Uncle Cole worries," Katie Jo said, going to work on the dishes, which were starting to pile up. "I think he just likes to have us close, so he can keep an eye on us. He forgets we're grown." She glanced out the kitchen window, spotting Zeke sitting on the porch, plate in his lap and cookie in one hand. "I forget sometimes too."

"I heard Drew had the same problem with Beth," Ciara commiserated, setting the bowl down and grabbing another. "His father died when he was eighteen, and he had to help raise all his younger brothers and her. I imagine Kit and I might fret too when Grace comes of age, sooner if wives continue to be scarce."

Out in the main room, a door slammed. Katie Jo leaned forward to try to get a peek at their newest customer.

Logan Bradshaw was ushering his son through the door. Likely the blacksmith was tired of doing all the cooking himself or maybe he just wanted to give his son a treat.

"The big table was finishing when I came through," Ciara told her. "Will you check on it after you get the new folks settled?"

"Happy to." She shook water off her hands and ventured out.

They were on their third round of diners when Harry returned.

"How's everything going?" he asked as she was wiping spills off one of the tables.

"Busy," she said. "But that's nothing new."

"What is new?"

She glanced at him. His head was cocked, so that a lock of mahogany-colored hair drifted down over one eyebrow. With his brown eyes alight, he looked as if he was sure she would say something inspiring.

She couldn't think of anything inspiring.

"Nothing, I suppose," she allowed, picking up her rag and heading back to the kitchen.

He followed her to the sink and leaned against the sideboard, where she piled the dishes to dry. She started washing her next set, and he took the dish she had dunked in the rinse water and began drying it for her. "Do you like working here?"

She cast him a glance. "You know I do."

"Why?"

The second dish slipped from her fingers. He caught it, rinsed it, and set about drying it too, all while peering at her with that same intensity.

Ciara pulled another batch of biscuits from the oven and frowned at her, as if she were just as perplexed by him.

"I like the bustle, I suppose," Katie Jo answered. "I like seeing what Ciara comes up with for menus."

Her friend grinned at her.

"And some of the customers are funny," Katie Jo allowed. "Just the other day, one asked if he could have sugar for his bacon and bean soup. Can you imagine?"

He chuckled. "That would be something." He held out his hand for the next plate. "What else?"

She scrunched up her face. "You trying to have a conversation, Harry?"

He beamed. "Yes, exactly. What do you think about the weather? I'm hoping for a late winter. How about you?"

"Rain holding off is always good." She shoved her hands deeper into the warm water. "Why do you want to have a conversation while I'm working?"

He shrugged. "Zeke told me you like it when people listen to you. I can't listen if you don't talk."

"There is that." She rinsed off a bowl and handed it to him.

"Am I doing something wrong?" he asked.

She sighed, letting her fingers bathe in the suds. "I can see you're trying to be nice to me, Harry. I'm just not sure how long it will last."

He straightened. "Understandable. I have to prove myself to you. Will you let me take you to church tomorrow and walk you home afterward?"

That really did seem like courting. Something fluttered inside her, fast as the wings of a dove, climbing into the sky. "That would be real nice."

"Good. Now, I'll stop talking and let you work. But I'm here if you need anything."

And he was. He moved tables so Zeke could sweep. He brought in more coffee beans for Ciara and ground them up for the morning. After that, he ducked out the back door.

"Did we finally scare him off?" Ciara asked, picking up one of the last of the gingersnaps and taking a bite.

Katie Jo spread her hands. "I told my uncle that Harry Yeager doesn't scare easily."

"You're right," he said, coming back through the door juggling an iron hook, screws, and a screwdriver. "That root cellar is too dark. I'm going to install this in a beam so you can hang a lantern if you like."

"I like this new Harry," Ciara said with a grin to Katie Jo as he clambered down the ladder.

Truth be told, so did she, maybe more than she should.

CHAPTER TWELVE

WHEN KATIE JO came down for breakfast Sunday morning in her gingham dress, Harry was already seated at the big table and watching the stairs, as if he couldn't wait for her to appear. Before she even reached the bottom, he had popped out of his chair and come to meet her, offering her his arm.

She raised her brows. "It's just across the room, Harry. I can manage."

He leaned closer. "It's not about managing, darlin'. It's about having the right to hold you close a moment."

Someone must have tightened her corset strings, for she was nearly breathless as she put her hand on his arm.

Zeke followed her a moment before striding past them to sling a leg over the bench. She and her brother had slept in a bed in the corner of the loft, the framed walls of the planned rooms looking like winter-bare trees around them.

Now Harry led Katie Jo to his place at the foot of the table.

"That's where you sit," she protested.

"That's where my lady sits now," he insisted, handing her down. He went to perch on the end of the bench closest to her. Jesse, at the head of the table, nodded good morning to her before reaching for his coffee.

Kit carried in Grace and put her in the tall, wheeled chair the Wallin family had given them. The baby had a wooden spoon in one hand, and she waved it at Katie Jo as well. Katie Jo wiggled her fingers to wave back. Grace chortled.

As Kit took his seat opposite Harry, Ciara brought in scrambled eggs, toast, and blackcap preserves, then took her seat next to her husband, with Grace in easy reach. Kit folded his hands and bowed his head.

"Dear Lord, thank you for this bounty and the beauty of your world. May they continue to be a blessing to us all."

Amens rumbled around the table. Grace rapped her spoon on the tray in front of her and offered them all a toothy grin.

Soon, Kit and Ciara had their heads together, murmuring. Zeke turned to Katie Jo. "Someone said there was church today. We going?"

"Most folks here do," Katie Jo told him. "I like it."

Harry nodded. "Me too. Levi Wallin has a way of talking. It doesn't feel like he's preaching at you."

She'd noticed that as well. "And Callie plays the piano real nice."

"Guess I'll come too, then," Zeke said, reaching for another slice of toast from the pile in the center of the table.

She only wished she'd thought to bring her fancy dress. Still, she'd been so careful with the apron that she was probably the only one who noticed dirt was starting to show along the hem of her gingham. She'd have to find a way to clean it off when she got home.

So, she, Harry, and Zeke followed Ciara, Kit, and Grace to the church after breakfast. Harry sat in a pew mid-way back, with Zeke on one side and Katie Jo on the other. One of the older men flapped his fingers to wave at her. She smiled before facing front.

Callie played a rousing hymn that had everyone singing. Harry's warm voice might not be as deep as Drew Wallin's or as high and pure as Zeke's, but she caught herself listening and had to hurry to sing herself.

Then Levi stood up to speak. The youngest of the Wallin brothers, he'd run off with Scout Rankin to seek his fortune in the gold fields, but he'd come home with a different kind of riches than his friend, a dedication to a calling.

"Autumn is moving along," he said, gazing out at his congregation. "Hay's in the barn. Apples are picked. Salmon runs are about petered out. The ground is starting to firm up, making it harder to mine. Thoughts are turning to what we can do to be ready for spring. It happens every year. There's a constancy, a commitment, to our work."

Around the church, folks were nodding. Zeke was watching him avidly.

"There's a constancy and commitment to our Heavenly Father too. The sun comes up every day. The seasons arrive more or less on schedule. The rain comes a mite too often for some."

A few of the farmers chuckled.

"So, why is it we find constancy so difficult? You've seen it. We stay home from church when the tide's low or the creek's high. We might only come for Easter and Christmas or any time there's fixing to be dinner served."

More laughed.

Levi held up his hands. "Don't get me wrong. I'm glad whenever I look out and see anyone looking back at me. But I wonder what keeps some from making that commitment."

Katie Jo glanced at Harry. As far as she knew, he attended services every Sunday when he was in the Landing, and he'd mentioned attending a church in Seattle when he had to be in town on the Holy Day. So, if he could make that kind of commitment, why hadn't he found a way to commit himself to a gal?

The thought stayed with her as services ended, and Harry escorted her and Zeke out into the sunshine with Ciara, Kit, and Grace alongside.

"Sure you don't want to stay for dinner?" Ciara asked as they headed for the inn. "I know you would be welcome, both of you."

Zeke looked to Katie Jo, brows up.

"No, thank you," she told Ciara. "We promised Uncle Cole we'd come home."

Zeke slumped.

She changed into her everyday clothes and folded and stowed her dress. Harry insisted on carrying her pack, so she let him. Zeke lagged behind as if already regretting leaving. She felt it too. Every time she walked away from Wallin Landing, the path home seemed longer, more narrow and dim.

"What's your uncle do when you're gone?" Harry asked as they followed the curve of the lake north.

"A bit of this and that," Katie Jo admitted. "He has traplines to check, and he has to care for the chickens and fend for himself when I'm not there. I think he'd rather be out fishing."

He flashed her a grin. "There's that constancy Levi mentioned."

She laughed. "I suppose it is. But being constant to God and being constant to a pastime is something else. He had a dream of panning for his fortune, and he let it go, for us."

He was quiet. Had she made him feel that he hadn't worked hard enough for his dream of finding a wife?

"I know about dreams," he murmured, gaze on the rough path. "I didn't have a family growing up, like you and Zeke. My parents died, and relatives took over the care of me."

"Relatives can be a family too," she said. "Like Uncle Cole."

He grimaced. "These relatives didn't want to let go of anything to help me. They saw me as an inconvenience at best and an unpaid hired hand at worst." He held out a hand and flexed his fingers. "I didn't get this strong going to school or playing with other boys."

Her heart ached. "I'm sorry, Harry."

He pulled back his hand and shoved it into his pants pocket. "That doesn't matter now, darlin'. What's important is that I'm finally in a position to start my own family." He winked at her.

Warmth rose up inside her.

Suddenly, Harry caught her arm, pulling her to a stop. His gaze was latched on the thicket they were passing, where the bushes rustled as if stirred by more than the breeze.

The branches parted, and a bear lumbered out onto the path.

Harry put Katie Jo protectively behind him. What had he been thinking to come this way without a gun? All he had for a weapon was her pack slung on his shoulder and his bare hands.

"Back away," he murmured. "Real slow."

She obeyed him, then turned slightly and motioned to Zeke, who'd come up after them, to do the same.

The bear squinted its eyes at them as if unsure what they were about and ambled closer. Harry tipped his head at the closest fir. "Can you shinny up that tree?"

She frowned at him.

Then she faced the bear and raised her hands over her head. "Yah!" she shouted. "Git! Go on! Blah!"

The bear stopped to stare at her.

She shook off Harry and stomped her feet. "Git, I said! You ain't welcome here! Yah!"

The bear turned tail and crashed back into the woods.

"You," Harry said, "are amazing."

She crumpled, and he caught her. Body shaking, she buried her head in his shoulder. He held her, stroking her back, telling her how brave she was, what a wonder, even as his heart beat a fierce tattoo. He didn't want to let go.

"Thanks, sis," Zeke said, pausing to eye Harry. "I'll go ahead and make sure it's gone."

He ought to protest. He thought *she* might protest. Instead, she just nodded with a sniff, and her brother loped up the path. Maybe Zeke was as fearless as his sister.

Silence settled.

"You take as long as you like," Harry said. "I'm in no hurry."

She pushed back enough that she could look up into his face. Her cheeks were red and shiny from her tears. "You really think that was brave?"

"One of the bravest things I've ever seen, darlin'," he told her. "And here I was worrying I didn't have a gun to protect you. You didn't need any protecting."

"I do, Harry," she said, lower lip trembling. "I can take care of myself and Zeke, but sometimes it all gets so heavy I just want to lie down and let someone else carry the load awhile."

"I can carry that load," he said. "I have plenty of experience."

Her frown was the merest crinkle of her brow. "Don't you get tired?"

"I used to," Harry admitted. "Seemed like everything was on my shoulders, and anything that went wrong was all my fault."

She nodded as if she understood. From what he'd seen of her uncle, she likely did.

"Then I came to Wallin Landing," he told her, "and I

found friends who'd stand by me, come along beside me. The load got a lot lighter."

"You offering to come along beside me, Harry?" she whispered, as if afraid to hope.

"Yes, ma'am. For the rest of our lives." And then he kissed her.

Harry was kissing her.

Katie Jo melted, like butter in a hot frying pan. His mustache tickled her skin, his lips firm and gentle. With his hands warm at her waist, she felt more precious than gold. She was trembling all over again, and she wouldn't have changed a minute of it.

He pulled back, eyes wider than she'd ever seen them, as if he marveled at the kiss too.

"I guess you're going to marry me," she said.

A grin split his face. "I guess I am."

She was pretty sure a similar grin sat on her face. "Well, who'd have thought."

"I would," he said. He tucked her hand into his arm. "Let's get you home, or, at least, your home for now."

Her home for now. She hung onto that as tightly as she clung to his arm as they followed the path north. She might not remember every lesson her mother had taught her or everything any of the Wallin ladies or Ciara had said, but she knew this much. When a gentleman kissed a lady, he was making a commitment to marriage. She might be going to the claim, but her home was going to be with Harry Yeager.

Her husband.

She kept glancing at him out of the corners of her eyes. He strolled along, steps cocky, as if he knew he'd just won the grand prize at the shooting match. She felt the same way. Harry Yeager was going to marry her—her! Not proper, petite Alice Dennison, not some fancy gal from Seattle who drank tea in a parlor with lamps that had fringe on them. Katie Jo McAllister had captured the handsomest logger in these parts. There was a story to tell their children.

"I need to talk to your uncle," he said as they approached the twin cedars and she caught sight of Zeke waiting on the other side.

"Why?" she asked.

He smiled at her. "That's what a gentleman does when he wants to marry a lady—ask the head of her family for permission."

"Oh." She dropped her gaze. "Well, I guess you should, then."

He squeezed her hand before letting her go. Slipping the pack from his shoulder, he offered it to her. "Back in a moment. Zeke." He nodded to her brother before continuing to the house.

"Where's he going?" Zeke asked, watching him.

"To ask Uncle Cole if he can marry me."

Her brother started, then frowned. "He ought to have just gone and married you. Uncle Cole will say no."

Her muscles knotted, and she couldn't move. "You think so?"

He nodded, but he took a step closer as if to protect her.

What was the world coming to? Her brother, protecting her? Harry Yeager, wanting to marry her?

They both waited, watching the house. It wasn't long before Harry came striding out. His face was red, his steps long and hard.

Her muscles freed themselves, propelling her to meet him. "What happened?"

He glanced at the house, jaw set. "Nothing's changed. I'll be back on Friday to walk you into the Landing."

Her uncle had come out and was watching them. Harry bent and pecked her cheek, then strode from the yard.

Katie Jo widened her stance and glared at her uncle. "What did you do?"

"What's best for you," her uncle said with a smile. "That's what I'm here for. To see to your best interests."

Katie Jo hitched her thumb at Harry's retreating back. "My best interests just stomped out of the yard. Why?"

"He asked for your hand in marriage," Uncle Cole said. "You've only known him a few days. It's too soon for such talk."

Katie Jo threw up her hands. "A few days! I've known Harry Yeager for months! It's only been the last week or two that he started showing interest."

"And that alone ought to tell you something, girl," her uncle insisted. "Old Joe came up to see me today. He tells me Harry's courted every pretty girl in miles."

She barely registered the fact that Old Joe had come all this way to talk to her uncle, apparently about her and Harry. Hearing about Harry's past courtships only brought her doubts rushing back.

She raised her chin against them. "What if he did? He didn't ask their kin if they could marry him. He asked mine."

"After they all found other men to marry instead. Makes me wonder what's wrong with that boy."

Katie Jo gritted her teeth. "He's hardly a boy. And I'm not a girl. You only have to be eighteen in Washington Territory to marry without your family's blessing. I'm two and twenty. Reckon I can make my own decisions on who to wed."

Her uncle stuck out his lower lip. "I reckon you can. But if you're smart, you'll listen to me. Suddenly, the fellows are noticing you, Katie Jo. Marty, Old Joe, Harry. Play your cards right, and you can do well by yourself and your brother."

Zeke took a step away from her. "Leave me out of this.

You marry who you like, Katie Jo." He shoved his hands into his trouser pockets and hurried for the house.

Uncle Cole nodded toward the chicken coop. "Roof started tilting while you were gone. You'll want to fix that before something comes hunting your chickens."

He went back into the house without another word, leaving her boiling harder than the water she heated for dishes.

Harry stomped his way back to Wallin Landing. How could Cole McAllister refuse his suit?

"Whole lot of fellers sniffing around my niece since she figured out how to wear a dress," he had said to Harry, the glow from the fire flickering in his beard. "Seems I should keep an eye out for the best of the best, and I'm not sure it's you."

The statement seemed to demand he beg. He didn't beg. Not anymore. The boy who'd had to wrangle for every meal, every kind word, was done with that.

"Katie Jo knows what I offer her as a husband," he told her uncle. "A claim, good work, a good reputation."

"Plenty of fellers hereabouts could say the same," he pointed out, setting the chair to rocking with a creak. "You want to marry my niece, you'll have to do better than that."

"Yes, sir," Harry had said.

Now he batted away an encroaching branch. What more could the man want? Money? There were few men as wealthy as Scout Rankin, and most were married. Piety? Somehow, he doubted Cole McAllister cared. And Katie Jo's uncle would be hard-pressed to find anyone who valued family more.

That was the main reason he hadn't argued further. He hadn't wanted to come between Katie Jo and her family. Family was precious, to be protected at all costs. If that meant biding his time and proving to her and her uncle that he had what it took to be a husband she could take pride in, so be it. He and hard work were well acquainted.

And this time, he was working for his future.

CHAPTER THIRTEEN

KATIE JO DID her best to keep busy the next few days. It wasn't hard. Her uncle hadn't done much of anything that she could tell while she and Zeke had been gone. Besides securing the roof to the coop, she had dishes and clothes to wash, eggs to gather, and a garden to tend. She managed to pick blackcaps with Zeke and put up a few jars of preserves, but the shelves in the house looked nothing like the root cellar at the inn. She didn't like thinking what would happen come winter.

Zeke tried to help, but, as the week wore on, his energy flagged and his skin paled. By Tuesday morning, he was curled up on the bed.

"I knew that trek to the Landing would be too much," Katie Jo said, pulling her hand back from his clammy forehead. "Best you stay here this time."

His face sagged. "But I wanted to come help!"

"Next time," she promised.

"You think Harry Yeager will help you nurse that sick boy?" her uncle asked from his place by the fire. He was perched on one of the rockers, peeling the bark off some willow to make a new frame.

"No one else is," she said, heading for the washtub.

He pointed his knife at her. "Don't you get uppity. You aren't the one shooting the deer to feed this family."

"Been a while since we had deer," she said, pulling down the cast iron frying pan. "Mostly I remember eating fish. Anything else, I shot."

He rose. "I'll get you a deer. A fat buck. Then maybe you can show your brother and me what you learned about cooking at that inn. We might as well get something out of the effort." He slung down his rifle and stalked out the front door.

The guilt wrapped its arms around her and squeezed. Uncle Cole had given up his entire life to see them raised. She knew that and was grateful. But shouldn't he be glad now that the work was nearly done? If she married Harry and took Zeke with her, Uncle Cole would be free at last to travel to the next gold strike, if that was still his dream. Why wasn't he encouraging her to move on instead of clinging to her?

By Wednesday, she couldn't stand the claim another minute.

"I'm heading in to check the mail," she told her uncle and Zeke over breakfast. She waited for the protest.

"Fix your hair first," her uncle said before shoving back from the table.

He was out the rear door before she could stop gaping.

"Since when did he care about my hair?" she asked aloud, hand going to the strands she'd shoved out of the way when she'd risen that morning.

"Seems he cares about a whole lot of things lately," Zeke said darkly.

Katie Jo dropped her hand and squared her shoulders. "Well, it makes no never mind. I'll be back as quick as I can."

Oh, but that promise was hard to keep. She looked all over for Harry as she came into the settlement, but James Wallin at the mercantile confided that he was out working with the rest of the crew, somewhere to the south. And of course, she had to stop by the inn and talk with Ciara. Then Callie showed up, and nothing would do but that she show them both how to make her anise cookies.

So, it was late in the afternoon when she returned to the claim. She thought her uncle might be out fishing, but she found him in one of the rocking chairs with Zeke on the bed with a book. He must have climbed out of bed at some point, or Uncle Cole had been in her garden, for a bowl of string beans lay on the table.

"No mail," she told them both. "I'll check again when I go back on Friday."

Uncle Cole nodded in her direction. "I keep hearing about this dress of yours. Go put it on, so I can see it."

Katie Jo glanced at the string beans, waiting to have their stems snapped off so she could boil them. "Now?"

"Now," he barked. "I'm expecting company."

Wonderful. This time when she aired out the house, she'd only be bringing in cold air. That wouldn't do Zeke any good.

"Then you don't want me in a dress," she told him as Zeke burrowed into his blankets like a rabbit diving for its hole. "Likely you'll want me to feed your friends."

"You can feed my friends," he said, moving closer and narrowing his eyes, "in a dress."

A moan came from the pile of blankets. Before her uncle could glance that way, Katie Jo put on a smile. "Dress it will be, then." She hurried to her corner and drew the curtains.

The space had always felt warm, safe. Now, it was as if her uncle's gaze was drilling through the fabric, watching her every move. What, did he think she was a doll he could dress up to show off? Well, he wasn't getting her best dress, the one she'd worn to Ciara's wedding. He and his friends could make do with the gingham, which she hadn't had a chance to wash yet. And she wouldn't bother with more than one petticoat.

She had already braided her hair down one side, so she pulled off the shirt, shucked the trousers, drew up a petticoat, and slid the dress over her head. She was finishing the buttons when the first knock sounded.

Knocks rang out several times over the next little while. She recognized Martin Delaney and Old Joe as well as three men who had visited her uncle in the past. Mr. Delaney and Old Joe took possession of the rockers, as if they thought it their due. The younger men pulled up the chairs from the table. No one paid any mind to the bed, where Zeke still hunkered out of sight.

Instead, they paid her far more attention than she liked.

"Come and sit with me," Old Joe encouraged, patting his knee as if she was his school-aged granddaughter.

"Supper won't cook itself," she countered, anchoring herself at the table and snapping the stems off the beans as fast as she could.

"She cooks too," one of the men said as if impressed.

"And cleans and washes dishes," Old Joe assured him. "Why, Mrs. Weatherly at the Wooden Rose Inn would be lost without her."

"She just doubled Katie Jo's salary," her uncle confirmed as Katie Jo dumped the beans into the tin colander and turned for the washtub to rinse them.

"So, she brings in money," another man mused. "I'd like to see how she looks without the dress."

The colander slipped from her fingers with a clatter of tin on tin. Surely her uncle wouldn't agree to that. Her heart was pounding so loud she could hardly think.

Uncle Cole rose to his full height and pointed toward the door. "Out. Now. And don't come back."

The other man stood with a scowl. "What did I do? You said you were looking for a husband for the girl. I just want to know what I'm getting."

Even as she swallowed the fear, Uncle Cole advanced on him. "My niece is a lady through and through. Anyone unwilling to treat her as such isn't worth her time or mine. Now, git, before I take down my rifle."

The fellow paled at what he must have seen on her uncle's face. He crammed his hat on his head and scurried out the door.

Katie Jo closed her eyes and whispered a prayer of thanks.

When she opened her eyes, Uncle Cole was glaring at the remaining four visitors. "Anyone else have a problem with treating Katie Jo like a lady?"

They all shook their heads. Old Joe went so far as to throw up his hands as if he were surrendering.

Katie Jo sent her uncle a smile, and he nodded to her. Whatever happened, it seemed he intended to protect her.

"He's not such a bad one, that Joe," Uncle Cole said that night. She'd managed to feed them beans, potato pancakes, and jerky, even though her hands kept shaking. "He's never made enough off his claim to do more than support himself, though. Patterson's a better choice when it comes to money."

"Which one was Patterson?" Zeke put in. Her brother had crawled from the bed after they'd left and helped her with the dishes. "The one with the squint or the one with the big belly?"

"Squint," her uncle said, not seeming to mind the description. "He has a boat, and he has to look into the sun a lot to get his bearings."

"It doesn't matter," Katie Jo said, setting the last dish back on the shelf. "I'm not marrying any of them."

Her uncle cocked his head, looking thoughtful. "You want them more muscled, like Harry Yeager?"

"Nicer," Zeke suggested before she could sputter an answer to the ridiculous question. "Harry's real kind to us."

Uncle Cole made a face. "Kindness never put food on the plate."

Katie Jo had had enough. She turned and braced her hands on the table. "I-am-not-marrying-them," she said, spitting out each word. "I'm marrying Harry, and that's all there is to it."

Uncle Cole rose from the table and patted her shoulder. "Just give it time, girl. We'll find you the perfect husband."

As if she hadn't already found one, in Harry.

It was a long week for Harry. The days were short enough now that he couldn't trek out to Katie Jo's claim to see her after work, especially if he hoped to have any time to finish his cabin and help Kit and Jesse at the inn, as he'd promised Ciara.

The latter proved easier. Oil lamps burning, the three of them could get an hour or two of work done after dinner while Ciara cleaned the kitchen and watched little Grace.

The upper floor of the old Wallin family cabin had held a small room at the top of the stairs, where Ma and Pa Wallin and later Beth had slept, with a larger, open room through a doorway to accommodate the Wallin boys on pallets. Now the stairs opened onto a corridor with three doors off it, one at either end of the loft and one in the middle. Drew had helped Kit break a hole in the roof and add a window for the middle room, so each had a source of light, and the chimney between two of the rooms helped heat the space. What was left was to finish the walls separating the rooms and move in furnishings.

"I appreciate the help, Harry," Kit said as he held a plank in place for Harry to tack up. "It's a little much for one man or even two." He nodded to where Jesse was painting the opposite wall.

In truth, Harry didn't mind. He appreciated both

members of the logging crew. Kit was quiet, like Jesse, but in a different way. He held his thoughts close, and Harry was always aware that more lurked behind those black curls. Falling in love with Ciara had helped make him open up a little more.

"What we do for love," Harry joked now, pounding in the nails.

Kit stepped back. "You'll be in the same position soon, if Katie Jo agrees to marry you."

Harry bent to lift the next board into place for Kit to pound. "Katie Jo already agreed. Her uncle's the stubborn one."

"Maybe you should court him," Jesse joked, swabbing a plank with white.

"Ha, ha," Harry quipped.

"I would have thought Katie Jo's uncle would want to see her happy," Kit mused, finishing his set of nails.

"He's not convinced I can make her happy," Harry allowed, waiting as Kit positioned the final board at the top of the wall.

"He just needs to spend time with the two of you," Kit said. "Anyone could see that you're smitten."

Harry grinned at him before whacking the first nail in. "I'm glad to hear *someone* thinks it's obvious."

"Well, I did think Alice Dennison had her eye on you," Kit admitted.

Jesse yelped, and Harry glanced back to find that his friend had splattered paint down his front. Mumbling an apology, he pushed past them and out the door.

Harry tilted his head to watch him thunder down the stairs. "If you ask me, Jesse is the one who's been smitten by the schoolmarm."

Kit raised his dark brows. "Somehow, I think those two are a more unlikely couple than you and Katie Jo."

After what felt like a week of working three jobs, Harry was glad to set the last chair in place in his cabin Thursday night. Then he shut the door and headed for the inn for dinner.

"I understand Drew's let you off so you can go out to meet Katie Jo tomorrow," Ciara said as she pulled the roast of venison out of the oven. John Wallin had shot a deer the day before, and this was their portion. "Tell her we just about have that second dress stitched, so we'll fit it on Saturday."

Harry plucked a honeyed carrot from the pot on the stove and popped it into his mouth. "What color is it?"

Ciara swatted him back. "The same color as her eyes. Which is?" She looked at him in challenge.

"The shade of blue of the sky above Mount Rainier on a sunny day," Harry replied.

She nodded. "We might make a suitor out of you yet, Harry Yeager."

As it was, he felt as if something was pushing him up the path to the McAllister claim on Friday. He stopped just outside the twin cedars, rubbed his hands down his trousers, made sure his collar was lying flat, and brushed back his hair. Then he pasted on a smile and strode into the yard.

She stood with her back to him, chickens trilling around her feet. Why hadn't he noticed those curves when they'd first met? Even in the dusty trousers and loose flannel shirt, she was all woman. Something washed over him—satisfaction? Pleasure? He didn't examine it too closely.

"Afternoon, darlin'," he said as he came up beside her. "You ready to come home?"

She jerked around, eyes wide. Then her smile widened too.

"Harry! Oh, I'm so glad to see you!" She threw her arms about him.

Harry held her close, relishing the feel of her against him. "Did you think I'd forget?" he murmured against her silky hair.

She pulled back and tucked a strand behind her ear. "Well, I thought you might find something better to do."

Someone better, more like. Harry shook his head. "No. Nothing will ever be more important than you."

It was an easy thing to say, and she blushed adorably. "I'll fetch my pack. Give me a minute to say goodbye to Zeke." She turned for the house.

"Zeke not coming this time?" Harry asked, pacing her.

"He's not feeling well," she said. "Maybe next time."

He could hear the doubt in her tone. "Maybe I should have a word with him."

She bit her lip and shook her head before answering. "I wish you wouldn't, Harry. It would just make him feel worse. He can't help it that he's puny."

Once Harry had gotten to know her brother, Zeke McAllister hadn't seemed all that puny. He had done his part in sweeping and cleaning the restaurant, and he'd been a big help at the cabin. Besides giving Harry ideas, he'd helped clean up around the pump and set up the grate in the hearth.

"I'll just pay my respects, then," he said.

This time, she didn't argue.

Zeke was lying among a pile of blankets on the bed. The boy levered himself up on an elbow at the sight of him. "Harry. Were you looking for me?"

"Sure was," Harry said, moving into the room. The sour smell of sweat met him. "I'm sorry to hear you're not feeling well enough to come in. I was looking forward to having your help on the cabin."

Katie Jo frowned at him, as if she thought he was trying to pressure the boy.

Zeke tried to sit up taller. "Did you get the window boxes in?"

"Sure did, but I could use your advice about what to put on the porch. A pair of rockers like you have here or a settee."

"Rockers," he said. "I know Katie Jo, that is your wife, would love them." He glanced at his sister.

"You worry about getting better first," she said, putting her hands on his shoulders and easing him back down. "Then you can talk about cabins and rockers and such."

He sighed. "All right. But I'll be in as soon as I can, Harry."

"I'll be waiting," Harry promised.

Katie Jo rose and led him out, picking up her pack from beside the door on the way. Slinging it over her shoulder, she started for the trees.

"No need to tell your uncle?" he asked.

"He knows I'm heading out today," she said without a look back. "If he wanted to say goodbye, he would have been here."

Harry caught up to her as they started on the path toward the lake. "I'm angry with him too, but it won't do either of us any good to alienate him."

She sighed. "You're right. Oh, but I could skin him alive! I don't know why he refused, Harry. He said something about waiting until we were sure. I'm sure." She glanced at him. "Aren't you?"

"Yes, ma'am," he promised. "In fact, I want to show you something before you start work this evening."

"Oh? What?"

"My cabin. Our cabin."

That blush was rising in her cheeks again. "I'd like that."

CHAPTER FOURTEEN

MAYBE IT WAS the thought of seeing the cabin or her desire to put distance between her and her uncle, but Harry and Katie Jo made the walk to Wallin Landing in surprisingly fast time, talking about anything and everything. Funny, but he didn't remember being able to jaw this long with anyone but her. She left her pack at the inn and told Ciara she'd be back soon, then followed Harry up past the Wallin claims to his.

The closer they got to the cabin, though, the more his shoulders tightened. "It still needs a little work," he hedged as they followed the base of the hill.

"I bet it's real nice," she assured him.

Suddenly he wasn't sure it was nice enough. He stepped into the clearing and turned to look at her.

She was gazing at the house. Did she see the care that had gone into the choice and placement of every log? The times he'd leveled the porch, until it was perfect?

"Here," he said, moving around her to hop up by the door. "I'm thinking of putting those two rocking chairs I mentioned to Zeke, so my wife and I can sit and watch the children playing."

She raised her brows, but she followed him as he opened the door.

"A table big enough for six," he said with a wave of his

hand. "I thought that might be a good number—Ma, Pa, and four young'uns. I only have four chairs for now, but there'll be time."

She trailed her finger along the edge of the stove, which he could only hope was a good sign.

"I put the pump inside, so my wife won't have to go out for water," he explained. "And there's a big root cellar under the house, with stairs going down, so she can put up what fruits and vegetables she wants."

Now her brows were coming down, and they kept lowering as he showed her the bedroom.

"One bed with trundle and the cradle for now. As the children grow, we can put beds in the loft. Privy's just down there, away from the creek, so it's easy to reach even in the winter."

She only nodded.

As they came back to the main room, she turned to face him, and she was as pale as her brother.

Harry's gut twisted. "Did I miss something?"

She nodded slowly. "You did, but I doubt you'll understand."

Harry crossed his arms over his chest. "Tell me."

Her eyes dipped down at the corners, and she raised a finger to tap his forehead. It echoed to his toes.

"You have a vision in your head, Harry, of the life you want and the wife you want in it. I have a feeling you know exactly how she acts, how she talks. I don't aim to squeeze myself into that picture. That's no way to live."

She had only spoken the truth, for all it hurt worse than slamming her finger in the cabin door, and she knew the moment he realized it. His eyes widened, he dropped his arms, and he took a step away from her, forcing her finger to fall.

"You don't have to squeeze yourself," he insisted. "You fit that picture just fine."

"Do I?" she asked, every part of her aching. "You set up everything the way you imagined your life, down to the number of children. Every piece of furniture is in place to suit that picture. Seems like I'm just another piece."

He shook his head. "You don't understand."

"I think I do," she said, wishing she was wrong. "You told me how you were raised, Harry. I can see how a family could be real important to you. It's important to me too. I remember the love my ma and pa had for each other. I'm pretty sure he didn't marry her because she fit into his plans. He married her so they could make plans together."

He threw up his hands. "Rearrange the furnishings, then. Paint the walls. Do whatever you please. I just want to marry you."

"You want to marry," she said, feeling as if she'd jumped into the creek in the middle of winter and dragged herself out, heavy and freezing. "There's a difference. Maybe you should sit and think a spell. I can find my own way back to the inn."

She made herself turn and head for the trees. She wasn't sure whether to be sad or glad that Harry didn't call her back.

This was all the fault of that stupid dress and corset. What had she been thinking to wrap them around her? It was like painting a piece of basalt pink. Everyone knew the color the rock was supposed to be—rusty brown, with a shiny spot here and there. She'd tried to disguise herself, and it had worked all too well. Harry was in love with the finery, not her.

So, she didn't change or fix her hair when she reached the inn. She walked into the kitchen, tucked her pack out of the way, and slipped an apron over her slouch hat, flannel shirt, and trousers.

"Probably a good idea to protect your clothes," Ciara said without looking at her as she stirred the soup of the day. "Chicken and dumplings and fish chowder for dinner tonight, though I'm already regretting the latter. Too much cream. It scalds the moment I step away from the stove. At least there's pumpkin cake and baked apples for dessert."

Katie Jo nodded, taking a sniff of the cinnamon-laced apples that sat on the sideboard. "I'll heat the water for the dishes."

She was clearing the big table when she heard the first complaints.

"What happened to that pretty gal?" one of the prospectors asked, picking his teeth with a sliver of wood.

"Bet she up and married," another said with a sigh.

Katie Jo eyed them. "You won't be seeing her anymore. You'll have to get used to me."

Another of the farmers, who was sitting at the table near the stairs, peered closer. "But *you're* the pretty gal."

Her cheeks heated. "Says you." She hurried for the kitchen.

"Trouble?" Ciara asked as Katie Jo plunged the dishes into the soapy water.

"Nothing I can't handle," Katie Jo assured her.

The kitchen door opened just then, and Alice traipsed into the room, black curls bouncing and frilly skirts bobbing. "There's a line around the inn. What are you cooking tonight?"

Ciara smiled at her. "I don't think it's entirely the menu. The local gents are aware there are two eligible ladies at Wallin Landing, and they're lining up to get a look at them."

Katie Jo blew a strand of hair out of her face. "Well, one eligible lady anyway."

Alice clasped her hands, purple-blue eyes gleaming.

"Oh, Katie Jo, did Mr. Yeager propose? I just knew the two of you were meant for each other."

Katie Jo spun to face her. "No, we ain't. You want him, he's all yours."

Ciara and Alice stared at her.

The front door slammed, and more voices rang from the room. Ciara dried her hands on her apron. "I'll go take their orders. Then, we need to talk."

Katie Jo nodded as her friend left the room. Alice came to lay a hand on her arm.

"I'm so sorry, Katie Jo," she murmured. "I didn't mean to hurt your feelings. I thought it was clear how Mr. Yeager felt about you. But I suppose I'm the last person to judge such things."

Katie Jo couldn't meet her kind gaze. "I'd have thought you'd have lots more experience courting than I do."

She squeezed Katie Jo's arm. "I was only courted once, and I thought surely he was the one. Everyone said so: my parents, my brother, my friends. He was the son of the most prominent family in our town, you see. I was very fortunate to catch his eye. They all made sure to tell me that too."

Katie Jo glanced up to find Alice's pretty face crumbling. "Did he up and die on you?" she asked. She couldn't think of any other way a fellow would leave someone as sweet as Alice.

"No," she said, lips trembling. "He found someone he could really love. It seems he never loved me. Everyone made sure I knew that too. Roland Cawthorn could do better. It was all my fault that I'd let him slip through my fingers."

Oh, the nerve of some people! "Well, I hope you told them all to go soak their heads!"

Alice's smile was as dainty as her stature. "I did something better, I hope. I left to seek my own way. That's how I came to Wallin Landing."

"Good for you," Katie Jo said, returning to her dishes and giving the first a good scrub. "Sounds like your groom and Harry have a lot in common. That Roland feller thought he wanted a different gal, and Harry thinks every gal is what he wants. He's looking for a wife, any wife. Then again, I suppose half the men in that room could say the same."

Alice put a hand on her heart. "Oh, surely not."

Katie Jo nodded, rinsing off a plate and setting it on the sideboard to dry. "Surely so. There are so few gals the best they can do is dream about one they'll find someday. They have her all cut out of whole cloth and ready to sew into something fine, just like Nora would a new gown. It isn't easy living up to their expectations."

"I imagine they would say the same," Alice pointed out. "A lady can afford to be picky in Seattle. That's the only reason I can think of that some young lady hasn't snatched up Mr. Yeager. He may have a certain type of wife in mind, but he is hardworking and kind."

Her throat tightened, and she swallowed as she set the next clean plate down carefully. "You favor him, then?"

Now Alice's eyes widened in what looked like alarm. "Oh, heavens no! Mr. Yeager is far too bold for me. I prefer a gentleman of a more studious nature."

Katie Jo snorted, toweling off her hands so she could dry the dishes. "You'll not find many of those in Seattle. Seems like every fellow came for the adventure."

"Just like I did." A dimple danced on either side of her mouth.

"Well," Katie Jo said, rubbing at the dish with the towel, "I hope you find it. The good kind of adventure, I mean. Not sure you'd want to meet a bear or a mountain lion or get washed out in a flood after a heavy rain."

Alice was paling. "No, thank you. I would not." She glanced out the door toward the main room. "By the way, I understand Mr. Hitchcock returned to the settlement today. Do you know whether he's eaten yet this evening?"

Now, there was a studious gentleman and one who would likely be able to take care of the fragile Alice. Katie Jo smiled despite herself. "I haven't seen him yet."

Alice straightened. "Ciara tells me he's turned the back room of the mercantile into his office. I thought that must mean he'll be needing to go somewhere to eat, like me."

"Unless he intends to cook over a fire on the lakeshore," Katie Jo allowed, stacking the clean dishes on the shelf where Ciara could reach them.

"I can't see him doing that," Alice said.

Neither could she.

Ciara bustled back into the room. "Talkative bunch tonight, but I finally got their orders. Table by the wall wants chowder for two. Table by the stairs wants chicken and dumplings all around. Table by the hearth has cleared out." She handed Katie Jo a shiny quarter. "Left a nice consideration too."

"I expect we'll be seeing fewer of those now that I'm in trousers again," she told her friend, tucking the coin into her pocket.

Ciara winked at her before starting to fill the orders for the latest diners. "Oh, you never know. Alice, what would you like? I'll set you up a plate while Katie Jo tells us why she and Harry are at outs."

Harry shut the door on his cabin and stepped back. It was a good house, solid, secure, practical in every aspect. So what if he'd built and furnished it without consulting Katie Jo? Most men he knew built their cabins before they had a wife, unless the wife had traveled west with them. Living on the claim was one of the requirements to prove it up. Hard to do without a cabin. He was pretty sure Drew, Simon, and John had had houses before they'd wed. He hadn't heard Catherine, Nora, or Dottie complaining.

Of course, Drew had remodeled his house after he and Catherine had started having children. Simon had built a new house for Nora up on the ridge. And Dottie had helped John design the library. Maybe he should have waited to finish the place until his wife could have some input.

And maybe it wouldn't have made any difference.

Mood dark, he shoved his hands into his pockets and stalked back through the trees. What was it about him that made all the women he'd courted turn away? He was polite. He tried to be kind. He was a hard worker. He'd more than proven he could support a wife and children. He'd seen enough ladies glance his way to know he wasn't hard on the eyes. There were few taller or stronger than he was.

He was a prince among men. Why couldn't he find his princess?

The ugly voices from his past argued with him.

Willful boy!

Anyone less would have buckled under the strain.

How stupid can you be?

Not nearly as stupid as they'd claimed. He'd learned to read and write and cipher despite them, and he'd made his own way in the world.

You'll never amount to anything!

Leader of Drew Wallin's logging crew, the most coveted position in his occupation in the territory. Months away from proving up his claim, a property owner.

Why would anyone love you?

That one hung in the air, taunting him. He had friends, neighbors who seemed to value him. But it wasn't that all-accepting love the Bible talked about. No one but his Lord had ever offered that, but at least he knew that was real.

Jesse was standing at the washstand when Harry came in.

"Thought you shaved this morning," Harry said, shutting the door behind him with perhaps more force then necessary.

Jesse frowned at him in the mirror, face lathered with soap. "What happened?"

"Nothing," Harry said, moving to the fire. "Like always."

Jesse lowered his razor. "Katie Jo didn't like the house."

"Oh, she liked the house just fine," Harry said, bending to retrieve another log and set it on the fire. "It's me that's lacking."

Jesse shrugged and went back to his shaving.

Harry glared at him. "You're not going to stand up for me?"

"Katie Jo isn't here," Jesse pointed out. "Wouldn't do any good."

Harry sank onto the chair by the hearth. "I just don't understand, Jesse. I have a good job, a claim I'll take title to shortly. I tithe to the church. I help with the school. Why can't I get a gal to marry me?"

Jesse shook his head before dipping his razor in the washbasin to clean it. "It's a mystery."

Harry sighed. "She said I had a picture in my head."

"You do," Jesse said.

Harry scowled at him. "Do not."

"Wife, four young'uns, cozy house in the woods," Jesse said. "You work, she tends the house and children. You're all happy all the time."

Harry snorted. "No one's happy all the time."

"True," Jesse said. "But they are in your picture."

The chair felt like a prison. Harry stood and paced the small space. "You think that's the problem? It's not my character or my accomplishments that are lacking? I can't get beyond a make-believe picture to see the real gal?"

Jesse shrugged again.

Harry stopped and watched him shave, mind humming. Katie Jo hadn't known him all that long, and, by her own admission, she hadn't gone courting before, so it was possible she'd misunderstood him. But he *had* courted before, with the same result every time—the lady he liked choosing another instead. This time, Katie Jo hadn't even said she preferred someone else!

Jesse had known him for years. They'd worked together, lived together, prayed together. He'd watched Harry court. If he saw the same thing Katie Jo did, Harry had to believe she was right.

Which meant he needed to change, because he still wanted to marry her.

"How do I show her I see the real Katie Jo?" Harry asked. "That she's the only one for me?"

Jesse toweled off his face before answering. "Is she the *only* one for you?"

"Don't start," Harry said, holding up a finger. "I'm trying to change."

"Good," Jesse said. "I like her. She'd be good for you."

"So, what do I do?" Harry asked. The question sounded very much like begging, but he found he didn't care.

"I don't know," Jesse said. "Courting scares the daylights out of me. You should see the fellows hanging after my sisters." He shuddered.

"What do they do?" Harry pressed. "The good things, not the bad."

"Follow them around like pups," Jesse said, coming to join him by the fire. "Fetch and carry for them. One even held the yarn so she could roll it." He shuddered again as if the memory was just too horrid to contemplate.

"She'd think I was crazy if I followed her around all day," Harry said. "And she doesn't need anyone to fetch and carry for her."

"Didn't her brother say you should listen to her?" Jesse asked.

"She doesn't talk! I can't listen if she doesn't say anything."

"Maybe she doesn't say anything because she thinks you won't listen," Jesse suggested.

There was that.

His friend clapped a hand to Harry's shoulder. "Dinner?"

Harry nodded, turning for the door. "Might as well. Unless Katie Jo agrees to marry me, I'll be eating at the inn for the foreseeable future."

CHAPTER FIFTEEN

EVERY TABLE IN the restaurant was filled as Harry and Jesse walked in, so they went straight to the kitchen. Katie Jo had her sleeves rolled up and her arms to her elbows in dishes. She didn't look at him.

"What will it be, Jesse?" Ciara asked, pausing with a spoon in a creamy-looking soup. "Fish chowder or chicken and dumplings?"

Jesse grinned. "Chicken and dumplings. Dessert?"

"Pumpkin cake. I had baked apples, but they're gone already."

"You need to make more next time," Jesse told her. "They always run out."

"So I noticed. But there are only so many apples in the area. You might remember that when you prove up your claim. You could find quite a few buyers for an orchard crop." She set about filling him a plate.

Katie Jo sloshed water on her trousers as she set the wet plate on the sideboard.

"I can dry for you," Harry offered.

"No, thank you," she said.

Jesse took his loaded plate and stepped aside, brows up as if encouraging Harry to act. He still had no idea what to do differently. He turned his gaze on Ciara.

Ciara stirred the soup.

Harry waited.

"Table by the stairs should be just about done," she called around him to Katie Jo. "See if they want dessert, will you?"

"On my way." She shook the water off her hands and vanished out the door.

Harry watched her go. Her shoulders seemed slumped, as if she were weary. He didn't think it was the work. She'd handled more, faster. He'd disappointed her, and it was weighing on her.

It was weighing on him too. He'd stopped trying to live up to other people's expectations. When had hers become so important?

"You are a skunk, Harry Yeager," Ciara said.

His gaze whipped back to her. She stirred that soup so fast he was surprised bits of fish weren't flying.

"Nice of you to notice," Harry quipped. "Can I have my dinner now?"

"I'm sincerely considering refusing," she said, eyes narrowing. "What were you thinking to treat Katie Jo so badly?"

He puffed out a sigh. "I didn't intend to treat her badly. I offered her a cabin in the woods. Most gals would have been pleased."

"It wasn't the cabin," she said, slopping soup into a bowl even though he hadn't told her which meal he preferred. "And you know it."

"I know it now," he said. "And I'm trying to find a way to make it up to her."

She plopped a biscuit onto the soup. Immediately it sunk in and began soaking up the liquid. "Try harder." She shoved the bowl at him.

He decided not to ask for dessert. "Yes, ma'am. If you have any ideas, I'm all ears."

"Stop telling her to wear dresses," Ciara scolded.

"I never told her to wear dresses," Harry protested. "I just told her how nice she looked in them."

"And stop complimenting her only on her beauty. A lady likes to be valued for more than how she looks on a man's arm."

Jesse had said the same. "I didn't think women would appreciate being praised for working hard."

"Everyone appreciates being noticed for their contributions," she countered. "Their character as well. You might start there. Show Katie Jo you really see her, and that you value her, just as she is. That's love, Harry, and Katie Jo has every right to expect it from the man she marries."

He would have sworn someone had lit a lamp. His whole world brightened. He longed for exactly the same thing. He couldn't expect it if he wasn't willing to give it.

Did he have what it took to share that kind of love with Katie Jo?

Katie Jo was sweeping up after the last customers had left when Harry ventured in through the front door. He'd taken his plate off to eat somewhere after an extensive conversation with Ciara, one she'd done her best not to overhear.

"He's thinking," Ciara had reported when Katie Jo had run out of excuses not to enter the kitchen, only to find that Harry had gone. "And all I can say is it's about time."

But just because Harry was thinking didn't mean he was thinking of marrying her, at least, for herself. She might have saved some gal sorrow in the future. That didn't mean she was set to be a bride. As it was, she had no idea what to say to him, more than she already had, so she kept her head down and hands busy sweeping the crumbs into a pile by the hearth.

"Let me help you with that," he said, bending just as she swept up to shove the pile into the fire.

The dust puffed into his face.

The broom fell from her hands. "Oh, Harry! I'm so sorry!"

He wiped a piece of dumpling from his mustache and gave her a smile. "Nothing to worry about. I'm fine."

She wasn't. Her dinner squirmed in her stomach as if it were just as uncomfortable. "Well, thank you for offering to help. I'm just about done here." She bent to retrieve her broom and nearly collided with him as he tried to do the same. He straightened and backed away, hands high as if giving up his rights. She started for the kitchen.

"I was wondering," he said, lowering his arms and following her. "Would you be willing to go for a walk with me tomorrow, assuming it doesn't rain? We have a lot to talk about."

She paused by the big table. "Do we?"

He nodded. "Starting with me apologizing. I'm sorry that I hurt you, Katie Jo. That was never my intention."

"I know that," she said, gripping the broom handle. "You can't help that you have that picture in your head, Harry."

"Maybe," he allowed. "But that doesn't mean I have to apply some made-up standard to every gal I meet, especially you." He bent and peered closer. "Could we start fresh and see where we go from there?"

He was so close, she caught a whiff of something musky and sweet. Her father had had a bottle of cologne, used only for special occasions like her mother's birthday. Had Harry put some on, for her?

Hope reached for the ceiling, begging to be set free. "All right," she said.

Harry's smile made her warm all over. For a moment, she thought he might kiss her, and she tingled from head to heels. But he leaned back with a nod and strode out the door.

She hardly slept that night.

But she didn't put on her gingham dress Saturday morning. Start fresh, he'd said, and she meant to. She was who she was. No sense posturing. She put on her flannel shirt and trousers, washed off her face in the basin, and ran her fingers through her hair. Good enough.

Little Grace was the only one visible as Katie Jo came down the stairs, though she could hear Kit and Ciara murmuring in the kitchen. The baby waved pudgy fingers from her tall chair. Katie Jo waved back, and Grace beamed as if she had been very clever.

What would it be like to have four little ones like Grace to tend to? Three boys and a girl, maybe. She grinned. Or four girls. It would be fun seeing how Harry dealt with that.

The smile vanished. Unless something changed, Harry wasn't likely to be the father of her children. At this rate, she'd likely never marry and *have* children. Best not to follow that thought too far. She went to set the table, anything to keep busy.

Harry and Jesse came in together just as she was putting down the last cup.

"Morning," Katie Jo said.

Jesse bobbed his head and loped for his place at the head of the table.

Harry sidled closer. "Need help with anything?"

"Nope," she said. "Just waiting for the food to come out." She couldn't help glancing out the window. The day was gray, the clouds heavy, but it wasn't raining. Yet. "Miss Dennison coming for breakfast?"

Harry shrugged as if to say that wasn't his problem. Jesse, who had straddled his chair, pushed back, setting it to rocking with a clatter of wood on wood. "I'll check on her." He was out the door before Katie Jo could stop him.

Ciara and Kit brought out platters of eggs and toast, and everyone fell to. Neither Jesse nor Alice returned before Katie Jo had finished eating. Harry shoveled the last of his food in his mouth as she stood, then rose to join her.

"Ready for our walk?" he asked.

Not even a little. But she couldn't disappoint him when he looked all wistful. He'd taken some trouble this morning, for his chin was clean-shaven, his mustache neatly trimmed. That mahogany-colored hair waved around his face as if carved by a master. He'd even donned a nicer waistcoat, one she'd seen him wear to church. He was dressed to impress.

He needn't have bothered. She'd been impressed with him for ages.

But he was waiting for her answer, once again as taut as a bow, so she nodded, and they set out from the house.

The Wallin family had cleared the trees along a strip of the lake and added a couple benches. A park, they called it. She wasn't sure why it was needed, when there were fields and pretty clearings all about, but it did have a nice view of the mountain when Rainier was out. Today, she was hiding behind a veil of clouds as Harry led Katie Jo along the damp grass.

"I want you to know," he said, "that I've taken your points to heart. You're not just any pretty gal. You're Katie Jo."

"Well, at least you know my name," she said with a smile.

Harry's brows drew down. "It's more than your name. You're a person. I understand that."

"Do you?" she asked as they neared the shore. "What do I want to do with my life?"

His frown deepened. "Marry, have kids. That's what all women want, isn't it?"

"Ciara just married," she pointed out. "She's already a mother with little Grace. But she runs a busy restaurant, and she's building an inn."

"Is that what you want? A business of your own?"

She kicked a rock into the shallows where it gave an enthusiastic splash. "Maybe. For the last few years, all I've thought about was how to make a way for me and Zeke to leave the claim. Other than that, I don't know."

Harry started laughing. "Well, if you don't know, how am I supposed to know?"

She joined his chuckle. "Sorry, Harry. That was a bad example. I was just trying to say that it seems a man and woman who aim to wed should know that sort of thing about each other. I know what you want—a home, a family, friends around you. I suppose I might want those things too."

His gaze was on the gray waters of the lake. "Yesterday, you mentioned that I have a picture in my head. Beth McCormick told me she thought I was too picky when it came to courting. I suppose she might agree that I was trying to fit every gal into that picture."

Her heart was starting to ache again. "You courted a lot of women, Harry, and you didn't marry any of them."

Now he bent and picked up a stone, then hurled it across the lake, so that it skipped once, twice, three times. "You're right. But it wasn't because they didn't fit my picture or because I couldn't be constant. It always seemed to me that I wasn't quite good enough. That's why they chose someone else."

"Oh, Harry." She put a hand on his arm. "I don't know why they didn't pick you. Maybe they just needed someone different."

He tipped up his chin. "Are you looking for someone different?"

She swallowed, releasing him. "No. You suit me just

fine. Or you could, if you cared more about me than the dress."

His brows shot up. "The dress? Why would I care about a dress?"

"Well," she said, dropping her gaze, "you only noticed me at Ciara's wedding, when I was all gussied up."

"Because I was blind, darlin'," he assured her. "But I promise you, I see you now. You could be whatever you want, and I'd support you." He winked at her. "You could always give Mrs. Volland a run for the money and put yourself up as a candidate for the school board."

"Me, on the school board?" The ache eased, to be replaced by another chuckle. "I'd be too quick to state my case. Can't you just see it? 'I don't care what your little darling wants, Mrs. High-And-Mighty. We're not funding a dance teacher.'"

Harry threw out his chest. "And you, Mr. Money-In-My-Fist, I don't take too kindly to you telling my son he can't smoke behind the privy."

"Smoke!" She slapped her knees. "No smoking in my house, Harry Yeager, you or your sons."

Harry spread his hands. "Guess it will just have to be our daughters, then."

The laughter shook her shoulders. "Or the cow. What about the cow?"

"Are you mad, woman?" Harry demanded. "The tobacco would stain the milk. I'll allow the pig to smoke. Might make the bacon tastier. But I draw the line at the dog."

"Fine," she said, laughing so hard the tears ran out of her eyes. "But don't you leave out the chickens. If I know them, they'll insist on having their own smoking room. Fran can be in charge of the matches. I don't trust Sadie."

"Done," he said, sticking out his hand.

She clasped it, and they shook, hard.

Harry released her to eye her. "Did you just agree to marry me?"

"Nope," she said, commencing walking again. "Just that *if* we marry, only certain barnyard critters get to smoke. I'm still not certain about you, Harry Yeager."

She might not be certain, but Harry thought she might be coming around. He would have been happy to stroll along the water as long as she wanted, but a wind swooped in from the north, bringing chilly raindrops that splattered down around them. Harry took her hand and ran with her back up to the inn.

Even after the short distance and part of it under the trees, her hair was hanging on either side of her face, and her skin was white and slick. He installed her in the rocking chair by the fire and went to fetch a towel from the kitchen. He could hear Ciara and Kit talking from the upper story. They must be working on the inn rooms.

"Grab one of the quilts and bundle up," he called as he pulled out a towel that had been close to the warmth of the stove.

She had one of the colorful quilts wrapped about her as he came back in. "Is this one of Nora's?" she asked.

"It was made by Mother Wallin," he answered. "She sewed every one of her children one plus more for company. Made the rug too, from what I hear."

She patted the braided rug with her toe. "I'd like to learn to do that. Course I'd need a whole lot of cloth, I suspect."

"Scraps, from what I understand," Harry said, handing her the towel. "Do you want me to…"

She snatched the towel away from him as if embarrassed by the thought. "No, I'll take care of it. Best you get warm too, Harry."

He bent until his eyes were on a level with hers. "I'm always warm when I'm with you, darlin'."

She rocked back in the chair, putting a distance between them. "There, you had to go and ruin it. I bet you called every gal you courted darlin'."

Harry frowned as he straightened. "No, I don't think I ever did." He winked at her. "Seems that one's for you alone."

And that put the color back in her cheeks at last.

They both helped Ciara and Kit around the inn until it was time to serve dinner. He kept remembering Ciara's advice about not complimenting Katie Jo on her looks, but how was he to avoid it when she looked so sweet up on her toes hanging the print curtain for the window in the middle room?

"You do that a lot," he said instead, touching up the wall with paint where Jesse had left it. "Help those you care about."

"That's what friends and family do," she said, stepping back to eye her handiwork.

"It's what friends and family *should* do," Harry said. "Not everyone remembers. You never forget."

Her cheeks were as pink as a mountain primrose. "You help too, like with the painting."

Guilt forced the truth from him. "I'm helping so Ciara doesn't have to hire anyone. If I work, she can afford to pay you a dollar a day. So, I guess I'm not such a good friend after all."

"I don't believe that," she said, turning to face him. "Look how you encourage Zeke and Jesse."

"Zeke, maybe," he allowed, forcing his gaze down to the bucket in his hand. "But Jesse? He's always there to listen to me when I have something I need to gripe about. What did I do in exchange? I arm wrestled him for the right to bring Alice Dennison out to the Landing, when Beth McCormick said that was his opportunity."

"And he ended up bringing her out anyway, from what I hear," she said. "I think you're being too hard on yourself."

"I don't," Harry said. "You and Ciara held up a mirror. I looked, and I didn't like what I saw. But if there's one thing I have, it's a powerful will. So I can change, Katie Jo. And I will. I promise."

CHAPTER SIXTEEN

A POWERFUL WILL, he said. Katie Jo could see that. He'd found a way out of his unkind childhood and become a man any parent would be proud to know. And now he wanted to apply that will to pleasing her. How could she not feel honored?

He stuck around that evening as the restaurant filled and refilled, even with rain starting to pound and wind beginning to howl. He dried and stacked dishes, even swept under the big table to the jeers of some of the men.

"You should have Mrs. Nora make you an apron, Yeager," one called.

"Better yet, a dress!" another put in.

Katie Jo had been loading two bowls for the latest customers. Now she strode back into the room and thumped them down on the table so hard the beef and vegetable soup sloshed. "It doesn't take a dress to see to the likes of you," she told the room at large, "just hard work and a willing attitude. You might try thanking folks instead of laughing at them."

"Thank you, Miss McAllister!" Logan Bradshaw's son grinned at her from his table by the stairs, and his father nodded his thanks as well.

Harry came to join her, lowering his voice for her alone. "Thank you, Miss McAllister. I can't remember the last time someone stood up for me in a crowd." He bent and brushed his lips across hers. She closed her eyes and, for a moment, just felt.

More hoots and hollers, along with a few groans of defeat, brought her head up. Instead of glaring them into silence, Harry slipped his hand into hers and led her back to the relative quiet of the kitchen.

Where she found it terribly hard to focus on her work.

Not so much the weather. It got busy with sheets of rain and even a fork or two of lightning. She felt the rumble of thunder through the planks at her feet. The main room emptied pretty fast after that, and it didn't refill this time. Even Alice, who had come for dinner later than usual, kept peering out the window, trying to judge a safe moment to cross the town center and reach her room in the school. Jesse finally accompanied her.

"May I escort you to church in the morning?" Harry asked as Katie Jo finished sweeping up.

"That would be real nice," she said.

He nodded to her and Ciara. Then he ducked out into the rain and ran for his cabin. Katie Jo shut the door behind him.

Ciara was drying off her hands with a towel as Katie Jo came back into the kitchen. "You've made quite an impression on that one."

"So it seems," Katie Jo agreed. But she was a little afraid of what would happen on Sunday. Working in trousers and flannels was one thing. How would Harry react when she insisted on wearing them to services?

Harry made sure to be at the inn early on Sunday, even though he had to shove a few downed limbs off the path. He wanted to keep his word to Katie Jo, but he also couldn't wait to see her again. In the past, he'd hurried to join her, afraid some other fellow would steal her away otherwise. Now, he just wanted to be the one to make her smile.

Kit was setting the table, and Grace was in her tall chair as Harry entered. The baby blew bubbles at him, then laughed.

"That's new," he told Kit.

"Katie Jo taught her," he said with a shake of his head. "We may hear it more than that other word for a while."

"No, no, no, no, no," Grace contradicted him.

Harry tickled her cheek before glancing at the stairs. "Katie Jo up?"

Kit tipped his head toward the doorway. "In the kitchen."

She was standing by the sink, hair tied back behind her head, wiping at a stain on her trousers. Light from the window bathed her in a soft glow.

"I'm not wearing my dress," she said.

"So I noticed." Harry nodded to Ciara, who was flipping griddle cakes. "Mornin', Ciara."

"Good morning, Harry. Breakfast will be ready in a few minutes. Will you bring out the preserves, Katie Jo?"

"Happy to," she said. "Give me a hand, Harry?"

She didn't usually ask for help, and he couldn't see why she wanted it this time. Fruit preserves weren't particularly heavy or challenging. But he followed her to the shelves on the opposite side of the kitchen. "Anything for you, darlin'."

Ciara frowned at him. What? He hadn't mentioned Katie Jo's looks, and he'd meant every word.

"You don't mind?" Katie Jo murmured, pulling down a jar of apple preserves and handing it to him. "Me not wearing a dress, I mean?"

Harry shrugged. "It's your decision. I know the Wallins dress in their best on Sundays, so I do the same. But I don't suppose God cares what we wear, so long as we honor Him."

She smiled as if the thought pleased her very much. He was still feeling wise as he walked her to church after breakfast. It seemed the rain had worn itself out over the blustery night, and the sun had rimed the remaining clouds with silver.

Katie Jo didn't seem to notice. She clung to Harry's arm as he led her to a pew. Men always outnumbered the women even here, but the area had enough wives now that the difference wasn't as large as it had once been. Even though their pew had room for another, she slid closer to him and kept her head down.

He wasn't sure why at first, but, glancing around, he found a few gazes aimed their way, including that of Mrs. Volland. Her long nose twitched as if she'd smelled something bad. Harry winked at her, and she flushed and looked away.

He wasn't sure why they were all aflutter. Callie Wallin, the minister's wife, donned trousers sometimes during the week for her chores, though she wore a dress to church. Katie Jo had done her best to make herself presentable. That should be good enough for anyone.

Jesse squeezed in beside them, pushing Harry even closer to her.

"Sorry," Jesse murmured. He twisted as if looking for another place to sit, but Callie began playing the opening hymn, and he collapsed back on the seat.

Harry couldn't mind. It was nice having Katie Jo close, feeling her body shift to reach for the hymnal, watching her tuck a strand of hair behind one ear. He already knew that hair to be soft and silky. He could imagine planting a kiss right where she'd tucked that strand.

He shook himself and focused on the service.

Afterward, he walked her out onto the wet grass. The children ran past for the school grounds, heading for the swings, their voices echoing.

"They need more of those things," Katie Jo said,

watching as a fight broke out between two of the boys. Nora went hurrying past as if intent on breaking it up.

"On the contrary," Mrs. Volland said, stopping next to them, her gingham skirts held up with one hand as if to keep them from touching the damp ground. "They should never have been erected in the first place. School is for learning, not cavorting about. When I'm elected to the school board, we'll have no more such nonsense." She smiled around Katie Jo at Harry. "I do hope I may count on your vote, Mr. Yeager."

He directed his smile at Katie Jo instead. "I'd rather hear what Miss McAllister has to say about the matter."

She smiled shyly at him.

"Miss McAllister is not a resident of Wallin Landing," Mrs. Volland said primly. "As such, she has no right to vote in the election."

Katie Jo frowned at her. "The Lake Union School serves every child in this neck of the woods. It's served adults too, in the past. Why wouldn't we all have a vote?"

Mrs. Volland tsked. "Perhaps if you had applied yourself enough to graduate from the school, you would know the answer to that."

Harry bristled for Katie Jo, but he couldn't exactly argue. Katie Jo likely had more time in school than he had had. Admitting that to Mrs. Volland would do neither of them any good.

"I'd like to know the answer too," he said instead. He glanced around and spotted Drew not too far away. "Mr. Wallin! Do you have a moment?"

Several heads came up—Simon, John, and James—but only Drew strolled over. As the patriarch of the Wallin clan and the acknowledged leader of both the family and the settlement, if the towering logger had been running for the school board, there would have been no contest.

"Mrs. Volland," he greeted in his deep voice. "Miss McAllister. How can I help?"

"Who exactly can vote in this upcoming school board election?" Harry asked.

"Anyone eighteen or older who lives within a half-day's walk of the school," he said.

"Male and female?" Katie Jo challenged.

"Yes, ma'am."

Mrs. Volland sniffed. "Far too wide a definition in my view. That's another matter I'll bring up when I'm elected."

"*If* you're elected," Drew said, "you do that. Just remember there will be four other folks on the board with you. They might have something to say about the matter as well." With a nod all around, he went to rejoin his wife.

"Well, then," Mrs. Volland said. "I hope I have both your votes." She hurried off to speak to James and Rina before either Harry or Katie Jo could respond.

"She sure doesn't have mine," Katie Jo said with a shake of her head.

"Mine either," Harry said. "No swings? What about a little play with all that learning?"

Katie Jo nodded. "When Zeke and I went, Mrs. Wallin used to read to us from adventure novels. It made me hungry to learn more about faraway places I might never see—Ohio, New York City, London, Egypt."

"I wish my teachers had thought to do that. I might have stayed in school more. Then again, I moved around enough that I wasn't in school long anyway."

She cast him a glance. "But you read books now."

"Sure do. Between Jesse and me, we've about worn out the copy of *The Last of the Mohicans* John Wallin has in the library."

She wrinkled her nose, and he bit his lips to keep from telling her how cute she looked.

"I know that one," she said. "Zeke had it a while back.

The ending is sad—two people who love each other never get to be together."

He should never have mentioned the book. He caught up her hand. "That won't be us, darlin'. I promise you. We're far more compatible. Why we even agreed to give the chickens their own smoking room."

She started giggling. The sound played like music along his skin.

He squeezed her hand. "Stay for the afternoon. I could cook you lunch if you don't want to eat with the Wallins. I don't have Ciara's touch in the kitchen, but I can put together a sandwich."

She pulled out of his grip, but reluctantly, he thought. "I should go. I want to see how Zeke's coming along."

"I could come with you," Harry offered.

She shook her head. "That's all right. A little time alone to think would be good for me." She winked at him. "Good for you too, Harry. I'll see you when I come in next Friday."

She headed for the inn.

Harry drew in a breath and let it out slowly. Friday would be a long time coming. The best thing he could do was keep busy. He went back to his and Jesse's cabin, changed clothes, and headed for his claim.

The clearing hadn't been immune from last night's storm. Fir branches littered the space, and the creek was running nearly to the top of its banks. Worse was the sight of his cabin. He must not have latched the door securely behind him, for it was swinging on its hinges.

He climbed up on the porch, which was piled with debris, and peered inside. Leaves and fir needles lay scattered across the planks and swirled into the hearth. Who knew what else might have taken shelter from the wind and rain? Not only would he have to clean house, he'd have to check every crevice for vermin.

He sagged back against the wall. What did it matter?

Without Katie Jo, the cabin was just a pile of logs anyway.

He blinked.

Without Katie Jo.

Not without *a wife*. Not without *a family*. Somehow, in the last few days, that picture in his head had changed. Now the woman bending over the table, working beside him in the fields, and cuddling close at night had taken on a form and a face.

One Katie Jo McAllister. No one else would do.

Now, he just had to find a way to prove it to her.

For Katie Jo, the walk to the claim seemed endless. Every step weighed, like the mud of the path was sucking at her boots. The wind came from the north, which was rare, pushing on her as if trying to urge her back to Wallin Landing.

She didn't need to wonder at the source of her feelings. She and Harry had made a new beginning, but hope shone brighter than a freshly minted silver dollar. He no longer seemed disappointed in her trousers and flannels or how she wore her hair. Maybe he was starting to see her for her.

She raised her head and pressed back against the wind. Perhaps, for a time, she'd judged herself on her clothing and hair too. Why? Her character was still the same. She was kind, helpful. She tried to do unto others as she'd want done to her. She knew how to worship her Creator. No friend, or husband, had a right to demand more.

Shoulders back and smile widening, she turned away from the lake and followed the path to the twin cedars and up to the door of the cabin.

This time, she couldn't help contrasting the claim to Harry's. She'd never really thought about how crooked the roof sat, until she'd seen how squared up Harry's roof had been. He had glass in the windows, flooding the place with light. And he had double the number of rooms and a real porch.

Inside, the differences were even more stark. Harry's cabin had a pump inside. He had a root cellar. He had a stove! Compared to her family's cabin, his was a palace!

Something stirred on the bed against the far wall. She had to remember that her cabin had one thing Harry's didn't. Her brother.

"Zeke?" she asked, pulling her pack off her shoulders.

Her brother crawled out of the covers, hair sticking every which way. His smile broadened. "You're back!"

She went to drop down beside him, setting the metal frame to protesting. "How are you feeling?" She put a hand to his forehead.

He shrugged her off. "I don't have a fever."

"Seems you're right." She lowered her hand. "Have you been getting up?"

"A little. Mr. Delany brought me some salmon. That helped."

"Nice of him," she said, tucking the blankets closer around him.

"Well, since he's going to marry you." Zeke spread his hands.

Katie Jo stared at him. "Marry me! Where'd he get that fool idea?"

Zeke's eyes widened. "I thought you'd agreed. Uncle Cole said it was a done thing. They're planning to get the preacher tomorrow."

She surged to her feet. "Over my dead body! Where's Uncle Cole?"

"Down at the Outlet fishing, I reckon." He grabbed her hand before she could light out. "Be careful, Katie Jo. You don't want to cross him."

"He's the one who should be worrying about crossing me." She shook off his hand and stalked out of the house.

What had her uncle been thinking to agree to a marriage without consulting her? He might think he was protecting her, but she didn't plan on hunkering in some half-built house in the middle of nowhere for the rest of her life. Even if Harry decided on someone else, she wanted more for her and Zeke, and she was about ready to take it, no matter what Uncle Cole said.

She smelled the briny scent a few moments before she sighted the shore through the trees. The Outlet brought fresh water from Lake Union and stirred it in with a healthy helping of salt water from Puget Sound. Waves lapped his boots as Uncle Cole stood at the edge, casting his line out into the swirling depths.

"What's this about me marrying Mr. Delaney?" Katie Jo demanded, stopping on the rocky shore and setting her hands on her hips.

He let the line play and glanced back at her. "He was the highest bidder."

She felt as if he'd slapped her. "Bidder!"

Her uncle nodded, then pulled his line back in. "Asa Mercer took money to bring brides from back East, so I figured I could do the same for you. You might be surprised what a gal is worth these days."

She was shaking at the very idea. "I determine what I'm worth. Not you, not anyone else."

"Even Harry Yeager?" he asked, casting off.

"Especially Harry Yeager."

He nodded again. "Good. Guess that means he won't mind when you marry Delaney."

"I," Katie Jo said, "am not marrying Mr. Delaney."

He yanked in his line, then planted the rod in the rocks. When he faced her at last, his eyes were narrowed to slits. She scuttled back like a crab, but he stalked after her until her back fetched up against a fir.

"You will marry who I tell you," he said, lowering his

head so that his eyes were on a level with hers. "I promised your ma and pa I'd take care of you and your good-for-nothing brother. That promise cost me everything. About time I got something back from it."

CHAPTER SEVENTEEN

KATIE JO WAITED for the guilt to creep up on her, smothering her with shame. Instead, her anger swelled higher than the tide.

"I didn't ask you to make that promise," she said. "I didn't hold you to it. But I don't see you made such a bad bargain. You had a home you didn't build, food you didn't grow or raise, on land you don't own. You spent most of your time doing as you pleased. I made this place a home. You want something from me? Take the house and land. Zeke and I are leaving as soon as he can stand."

If he was impressed with her show of bravado, he didn't show it. "No," he said, grabbing her arm. "You're going to marry Delaney. He's agreed to move in with you and Zeke, so you can keep cooking and cleaning and caring for the critters. This money will finally win me free."

Anger burned so fiercely she was surprised it hadn't set his hair on fire. "Let go of me."

For a moment, she thought he'd refuse. Red crept up from the neck of his flannel shirt and into his face above his beard; his breath came hard and fast. Then he yanked back his arm and stormed off to fetch his fishing rod.

She ran. Dodging around firs and slipping on fallen leaves. She plunged through the rear door and shot the bolt. As Zeke stared at her, she dashed to the front door to do likewise. It wouldn't be enough to keep their uncle out if he started kicking, so she shoved her mother's chest over it and tipped up the table as well, then wrestled the sideboard over the rear. Nothing she could do about the windows, but the slats might take him a while to hack off, if he could find where she'd stored the axe.

Zeke had scrambled out of bed as she was working. "What happened? What's wrong?"

"I won't marry Delaney," she said, eyeing the fireplace and wondering whether she ought to stop it up too. No, she ought to build a bigger fire. That would keep her uncle or anyone else from trying to climb down the chimney.

Zeke drew closer and dropped his voice as if he thought their uncle had his ear pressed to the door even now. "You figuring to ride it out until he relents?"

She straightened from adding wood to the grate. Panic was gnawing its way through the anger, like a beaver intent on toppling a tree. "I was. Not a good plan, was it? We only have so much food and wood. He'll break through a window or a door soon enough or starve us out."

Zeke studied the front door a moment. "Can you hold out until morning?"

She frowned. "Probably. Why?"

His gaze came back to hers. "Because that's how long it would take me to reach Wallin Landing and bring help."

She clutched her brother's shoulder, so thin under the cotton shirt. "No, Zeke! You won't make it by dark. You can't be out in the woods then. It's not safe. And you're sick. I don't know if you can walk that far right now."

He straightened to his full height. When had he been able to look down at her? His green eyes blazed. "I can walk as far as I need to walk to keep you safe. You've protected me all my life. Now, it's my turn."

Harry always enjoyed Sunday afternoons at Wallin Landing. As a member of Drew's logging crew, he was invited to take part in the family dinner at the hall next to the church. Every member of the Wallin family and their friends, from Drew to baby Grace, gathered at the long table down the middle of the hall, while every family contributed to the foods piled on the tables against the windows that looked out on the forest. Beth and her husband often came in from Seattle, and so did Scout Rankin and his bride Ada.

The adults took turns playing games with the children, giving the other mothers and fathers a break. Today it had started with blind man's buff and progressed to drop the handkerchief. All the Wallin children sat in a circle facing each other while Victoria, the only daughter of James and Rina Wallin, minced her way around behind them, fluttering a lace-edged handkerchief at their shoulders. Harry put his elbows on the table and leaned back on the bench to watch.

"She's quick," Jesse said beside him as she dropped the handkerchief behind one of her cousins and took off running. "Smart too. Little Davy won't catch her, so she'll get to stay queen for another turn."

Harry nodded as Victoria passed her spot in the circle and turned smugly to confront her younger cousin, who slumped in defeat. Would he have children one day, dashing about and playing tricks on each other?

Only if Katie Jo was their mother.

Miss Dennison had been invited to join in the fun as well. She sat at one end of the table. Everyone had gone out of their way to speak to her, encourage her. But, at that moment, Harry caught her gazing down at the hands clasped in the lap of her pretty rose-colored gown, a somber expression on her face.

He tipped his chin in her direction. "What's wrong with the schoolmarm?"

"Nothing," Jesse said, forking up a mouthful of pumpkin cake Ciara had contributed. "She's perfect as far as I can see."

Harry turned to eye him. "That right? Perfect?"

Color was climbing in Jesse's cheeks. "Smart. Sweet. Kind. You know."

Harry nodded. "Oh, I know. I just didn't think *you* knew." He leaned closer. "So, what's stopping you from going down there and asking if she'd like to take a walk by the lake?"

Jesse pointed his fork in her direction. "Them."

Someone had invited Dixon Hitchcock and Logan Bradshaw to take part in the festivities today. Both the lawyer and the blacksmith had stopped beside the schoolmarm, the latter with his son clinging to his hand. He was a bright-looking lad, with dark-brown hair and a winsome smile he'd likely inherited from his mother. Miss Dennison smiled politely and spoke to the boy, who hung his head and tried to dig his toe into the planks of the floor.

"You can take them," Harry said, returning his gaze to his friend. "You're taller than either of them, you're more patient, and you have more experience with children."

"The blacksmith has a child," Jesse pointed out.

"*A* child," Harry countered. "You've helped raise nine children."

Jesse shook his head, scraping the last of the cake off his plate. "She's not the gal for me, Harry. I'd never be able to keep up. But that's okay. You can look at a wildflower without wanting to pick it and take it home with you."

"And maybe that wildflower will only grow tall if it's planted in your front yard," Harry argued.

"Maybe," Jesse said, slinging a leg over the bench to

rise. "But I don't like the odds." He strode to the food table with his plate, likely looking for seconds.

Twilight had fallen by the time they all headed back toward their homes. Catherine and Drew strolled along, one child up over his shoulder, one of his hands holding hers. A wave of longing swept over Harry. Friday was too far away. Maybe he'd beg Drew for another day off and head up to the McAllister claim mid-week, just for a moment to talk to her.

"What's that?" Jesse asked, nodding toward their cabin.

Something that looked like a pile of washing was draped on the stoop. Frowning, Harry strode forward. The wash pile stirred, and a blond head poked out, green eyes blinking.

"Zeke!" He was at the boy's side in two steps. "What happened? Where's Katie Jo?"

Even in the dim light, he could see that the boy's eyes were glazed. His breath wheezed out, shallow and faint.

"He can't hear you," Jesse said.

Harry bent and scooped Katie Jo's brother up in his arms.

"Fetch Catherine," he told his friend. "I'm taking him to the dispensary."

Jesse nodded and ran.

Harry held Zeke close and moved down the path back through the village center to where Catherine's dispensary was located on the road to Seattle. He pushed against the door, but it wouldn't give. Figures. She was smart enough to lock up the life-saving medicine when she wasn't around to tend it.

"Harry!" She came hurrying up, Jesse right behind. Despite the rush and having spent the afternoon with a room full of children, not one pale hair was out of place.

"What's happened?" she asked.

"We found Katie Jo's brother, Zeke, like this at the

cabin," Harry said as she unlocked the door. "I don't know how long he lay there before we arrived."

"Jesse, light a lamp," she said, bustling into the room. "Harry, set him down on the examining table. Gently."

Drew had built the small cabin for his wife just before they'd married, and his workmanship showed in the warm woods and precise joints. Shelves lined most walls, filled with the tonics and equipment she used to help people. The desk under the window held a journal and pen for her to note progress, and a long polished wood table stood in the center of the space, where she could examine her patients.

Harry lay Zeke down on the slab, then stepped back to give Catherine room. A part of him wanted to wake the boy, demand to know Katie Jo's whereabouts, but Zeke had enough to deal with without adding to his troubles.

"Zeke?" Catherine called, tapping his cheek. "Zeke, can you hear me?"

"He's a little hard of hearing," Harry told her. "You might have to talk louder and stand where he can see your lips."

Catherine repositioned herself and raised her voice. "Zeke!"

Zeke shifted on the table and moaned.

"Sal volatile, Jesse," she said. "That brown bottle on the second shelf by the window."

Jesse located it and handed it to her. Unstopping it, she waved it in front of Zeke's nose. Even Harry could smell the harsh scent of ammonia.

Zeke recoiled, then started coughing. She eased him up until he was sitting.

His eyes popped open, and his gaze swung from Catherine to Harry.

"Trouble," he croaked. "Katie Jo's in trouble."

Harry fought the urge to shake the rest out of him. "What kind of trouble, Zeke?"

He visibly swallowed, and his voice came out stronger. "Uncle Cole promised her in marriage to an old codger up our way. She would have none of it. She barricaded herself in the house, but it's only a matter of time before he breaks in."

"Surely he wouldn't force her to marry," Catherine protested, blue eyes wide.

Zeke's gaze met hers, then dropped. "No, ma'am. Katie Jo is pert near his size, and she can handle herself. He'll just beat me until she agrees."

Harry gritted his teeth so hard his jaw hurt.

Catherine put her arm about Zeke's shoulders. "No, he won't. You'll be staying here with us."

"You do that, Catherine," Harry said, backing for the door. "Zeke, you did well coming to fetch me. Don't you worry. I'll ride out and bring Katie Jo back to you."

Catherine rounded on him. "Harry, no! You can't go tonight. There's no moon. It would be dangerous for you and the horse."

He met her gaze. "You don't understand. I can't leave her up there, fearing."

She looked to Zeke. "Does Katie Jo know where you've gone, Zeke?"

He nodded.

She returned her gaze to Harry's. "Then she knows her uncle can't do anything tonight." She swiveled to eye his friend. "Jesse, go tell Levi what's happened. If someone comes asking him to perform a marriage ceremony, he can find excuses to refuse until we have Katie Jo back with us as well."

"Ma'am," Jesse said before striding out.

Harry paced from the farthest shelves to the door and back, trying to find a way to counter her logic. "I won't take a horse. I'll walk."

"And face bear and lynx and who knows what else is out hunting tonight?" Catherine shook her head and finally managed to dislodge a lock of hair. "Think, Harry. You're no good to her dead."

He gripped the side of the table and met her gaze straight on, heart thrumming a powerful beat in his chest. "I'll go mad waiting."

"Then I'll just have to keep you busy," Catherine said primly.

She did just that, no matter the fear that tore at him. She had him help Zeke to stretch out on the table, then hold his shoulders while she asked the boy this and probed at that. Zeke turned paler all the while.

"You eaten today?" Harry asked as Catherine went to pull a book off the shelf beside her desk and page through it.

"A little at breakfast," Zeke admitted. "I wasn't all that hungry."

Catherine must have heard the statement, for she glanced up and met Harry's gaze. "See if Ciara has any eggs left from today, Harry. Ask her to scramble them with some cheese. And bread with butter and jam wouldn't hurt."

He stepped away from Katie Jo's brother, turned his back to face Catherine, and lowered his voice. "What do you think ails the boy?"

"Still considering," Catherine said.

And so he found himself running between the inn and the dispensary as the night wrapped the Landing in darkness. Catherine had been right. He wouldn't have made it to the McAllister claim in time, and he might have lost his way completely in the dark. But the ache inside him—to see her, to touch her, to know she was safe and happy—only grew deeper as he brought the food back for her brother.

Ciara, of course, had demanded to know why he needed the food to begin with. So he had had to explain about Katie Jo and Zeke a second time.

"But you'll go after her," Ciara had said, glancing up from where she had been cooking the eggs. "You won't leave her alone with that man."

"I'll fetch her," Harry had said. "I promise. But I can't go until morning."

She had nodded with a sigh.

Now he watched as Zeke wolfed down Ciara's offering along with guzzling a tall glass of water. Catherine watched too, head cocked. Harry hadn't had time to return the plate and utensils when Drew arrived. His boss must have alerted his other brothers, for Simon, James, and John had followed him, along with Jesse and Kit. Harry had to step outside and explain everything a third time.

"We'll go first thing in the morning," Drew said when Harry finished. He glanced around at the others. "Harry, Jesse, Simon, and I will go on horseback. The rest can follow by foot."

Morning, like Friday, seemed a very long time coming.

Zeke was curled up on his side when Harry went back into the dispensary. He glanced at Catherine, who put a finger to her lips and beckoned him closer.

"He was worn out, poor dear," she murmured. "I begin to suspect the culprit, but I'll know more when you bring Katie Jo to me and I can ask her a few questions. I'll stay with Zeke tonight. Why don't you try to get some sleep, Harry?"

He shook his head. "I can't sleep. You go on home. I'll come for you if Zeke needs you."

She studied him a moment, as if he were one of her elixirs. "You've changed."

"I hope you're right," he said. "I have a lot of work to do if I'm to be the husband Katie Jo McAllister deserves."

Her smile hovered. "You must care about Miss McAllister a great deal."

"I love her." The words came out deeper than he'd

intended, and he cleared his throat. "I love her. And I aim to make her my wife."

She lay a hand on his arm. "I'm very glad to hear that, Harry." Leaning closer, she pecked his cheek. "She is a very fortunate young lady."

Still smiling, she left him.

Harry took her place at the desk. Leaning back in the chair, he turned his gaze to the sturdy crossbeams of the ceiling. Instead of weathered logs, he saw Katie Jo's face, alight with wonder, laughing about giving the chickens a smoking room.

"Stay strong, darlin'," he whispered. "Don't give up on me."

CHAPTER EIGHTEEN

Z EKE SLEPT, AND Harry might have dozed, but he was in the barn saddling Lancelot before the sun had poked up over the Cascades. When Drew came in a few moments later, Harry had Percival saddled as well. His boss merely nodded his thanks, and they mounted and cantered out to meet Simon and Jesse, up on Simon's two horses. He sighted Catherine picking her way across the clearing for the dispensary and the other men gathering by the inn to follow the horsemen.

"Lead the way," Drew told him.

Harry urged Lancelot out of the clearing for the north.

They covered the ground quickly, but every second dragged. Lancelot balked when Harry tried to nudge him faster. Powerful horse or not, the trail was only so wide, and Lancelot had to jump over a fallen log and detour around deeper puddles. Branches whipped Harry's face and clung to his coat. Dew dropped to wet his hair. Nothing mattered but getting to her.

Finally, the twin cedars came into view. Harry raised a hand and reined in. The others followed suit.

"The clearing with the McAllister cabin is just beyond here," he told them. "It would be best if I go in alone. Wait for my signal before following."

Drew eyed him. "You sure?"

"Her uncle generally treats me with respect," Harry told him. "Maybe I can talk him out of this course."

"Then we'll wait," Drew said, resting a fist on the saddle horn. "Call when you need us."

Jesse and Simon nodded.

Harry dismounted, threw his reins to Jesse, and walked through the cedars.

The clearing stood empty. The chickens must be still in their coop; he could hear stirring from that direction. A trickle of smoke came from the cabin's chimney. He could only hope that meant Katie Jo had kept warm through the night. Of course, that likely meant her uncle had been forced to sleep out. Nothing like poking an already-grumpy bear, but there was nothing for it. He started forward.

Cole McAllister stepped out from around the side of the cabin and stared at Harry down his rifle.

"That's far enough, Yeager."

"Mr. McAllister," Harry acknowledged, pulling up short. "Zeke came to find me. Seems there's been a misunderstanding."

"There's always a misunderstanding with that boy," Katie Jo's uncle said. "He probably thought he heard something of concern. But we're fine. Shame you came all this way for nothing."

"I didn't come all this way for nothing," he said. "I came here for the woman I'm going to marry."

McAllister shook his head. "Sorry, son. You're too late. She accepted someone else."

"Did not!" Katie Jo's voice was a roar from the house. "Did not, and never will!"

Harry couldn't help his grin. "Sounds like your niece and I understand each other well enough."

He cocked the rifle. "The only thing you need to understand is that you're leaving now, and you ain't welcome to come back."

He couldn't rush him without the risk of getting shot. Even if he signaled the others, McAllister might shoot him or one of them. But he thought he knew a way forward.

Harry raised his voice. "Don't you fear, Katie Jo McAllister. I see you. The real you. The one who is kind and hopeful and leaves everyone better off than they were before. I know who you are. I love you. And I'm coming for you."

Katie Jo pressed her back against the front door and her fingers against her lips. Harry Yeager loved her. She ought to doubt, but she didn't. Her lips trembled as her fingers dropped. Harry loved her, just as she was, and he was coming back for her. She felt as if she had wings bigger than an eagle's and could fly right up into the sunlight.

"Don't you listen to him, girl," Uncle Cole called from the yard. "He hightailed it out of here. You're marrying Delaney, and that's that."

"No," she shouted through the door. "I'm not. And the sooner you get that through your fool head, the better off for both of us."

She bit her lip. Had she just called her uncle a fool? Oh, that hadn't been very smart. She'd already spent a sleepless night waiting for him to beat down the door or break open a window. Maybe he'd thought Mr. Delaney would mind if he left bruises on her. But her uncle would be plum out of patience by now. She listened, counting off the seconds.

When his voice sounded, it was right up against the door. She jerked back.

"You can't stay in there forever," he said, "and you know it. I'll give you a quarter hour to consider your options, then I'm coming in after you. And if that feller of yours returns before then, I'll shoot him for trespassing."

She swallowed as the sound of footsteps faded away. She didn't doubt him either. He would hurt Harry if Harry got between him and his goals. Harry might not be as frail as Zeke, but she would never live with herself if he was harmed because of her. She had to trust he would return before her uncle found a way to force her to say *I do* to anyone but him.

A quarter hour, he'd said. She could feel every second like a clock ticking. She dashed to her corner and shoved everything she cared about into her pack, until clothing sprung from the top and the sides bulged. She found Zeke's pack and stuffed in whatever she could find he might want. If she was leaving the claim forever with Harry, might as well take as much as she could now. A shame she couldn't carry her mother's chest or its contents, but she was certain her mother would applaud her initiative. She'd understood leaving a home in the East to be with the man she loved.

"Time's about up," her uncle shouted from the yard. "You could make it a whole lot easier on yourself by coming out now."

"I'm not ready," she called back. "I have to put on a dress if I'm getting married."

"Delaney won't care about a dress."

"He might," she said, laying more kindling on the fire. The flames licked out greedily. "I was in a dress the last time he saw me. He might go back on the deal if he sees me in trousers again. Best I fix my hair too. It will take a bit to heat the curling iron. Ciara gave me one last time I was down." That was another half-truth. She and Ciara had only talked about curling irons when she'd gone in for the mail last week. But anything to give Harry time to return.

"Will you stop your primping?" her uncle demanded. "Delaney already paid."

"It's *my* wedding day. I want to look pretty." She added

logs to the fire, until she could no longer stand in front of it for the heat.

"Times up. Get out here, now!"

She dusted off her hands and hefted her pack and Zeke's, then went to remove the table and chest from the door. "All right. I'm coming."

She flung open the door and stepped out into the yard. Her uncle was a few feet away, gun up and wariness etched on his lean face.

"I'm out," she said, moving to one side so he could get a clear view into the cabin. "But you better go in if you want to save the house. That fire's about to take everything."

His mouth hung slack a moment, then he shoved past her for the cabin.

Once more, she ran. Packs bumping against her back, legs pumping against the dirt, she pelted for the cedars. She hadn't crossed half the distance before horses exploded through the opening, Harry at the head and the two oldest Wallin brothers and Jesse right behind. Following were James and John Wallin and Kit Weatherly. She jerked to a stop as they surrounded her.

"Quick," she said, heart pounding. "He's busy, but he'll be out before you know it."

Harry jumped down from his horse and folded her close. He felt as good as a warm blanket on a cold winter morning. Then he leaned back, braced his hands on her waist, and lifted her up onto the saddle. "Can you ride?"

"Nope," she said, clutching at the saddle, legs dangling on one side. "Never had call."

"I'll skin you alive!" The shout echoed through the yard, setting two of the horses to prancing. As she caught her breath, her uncle stormed out of the house, leather shaving strap in his hands, only to pull up short, gaze darting around at the seven men and four horses.

Harry kept his hand on hers on the saddle, solid, sure. Simon Wallin and Jesse cocked rifles.

Drew leaned forward in his seat to face her uncle. "Miss McAllister is of age. She's coming with us. I understand she's the closest kin to young Zeke McAllister. My wife is treating him for injuries sustained on this claim. He will be staying with us until he's well. I'll let him decide where he wants to go after that."

She sent a prayer of thanks heavenward. Surely no one would argue with Drew Wallin.

Her uncle tried. "You got no right!" He took a step closer. "They're my brother's children. I raised them."

She'd had enough. "You used us! I see that now. You did as little as possible to keep your promise to your brother, all the while making me feel as if it were somehow all my fault. And you'll continue unless I put some distance between us. You can have the claim and anything that's on it. I want no part of it or you."

Uncle Cole took another step forward, eyes focused on her. "Get off that horse."

Harry let go of her and strode to meet him. "Leave my bride alone. You have a problem with her or her brother, you'll be dealing with me from now on."

Uncle Cole's face hardened. "Fine. You want them? Take them. Don't come running to me when you find they're more trouble than they're worth."

She nearly sagged on the saddle.

"Go to Wallin Landing," Drew ordered Harry. "We'll make sure Mr. McAllister is settled on his claim."

She wasn't sure what the logging boss intended, but Harry didn't argue. He turned his back on her uncle, and Uncle Cole raised his strap.

"Watch out!" Katie Jo cried, pointing.

Harry whirled and smashed his fist into her uncle's jaw. Uncle Cole dropped like a sack of flour that had been left out in the rain. She couldn't help the cheer that bubbled up.

"Yes!"

Harry's swagger had never been more evident as he returned to the horse. He swung himself up in front of her. "Let's get you home, darlin'."

She wrapped her arms around him and leaned her cheek against his back. With Harry, she was already home.

Harry turned his face to Heaven and offered his thanks. For a moment, he hadn't been sure he could help her escape without someone getting hurt. As it was, he could only hope Drew and the others would talk some sense into her uncle. He didn't want her to have to look over her shoulder for the rest of her life.

"You all right?" he asked as he let the horse amble toward the lake.

She snuggled into his back like it was a feather pillow. "I'll be fine." Then she stiffened, and cool air rushed between them. "How's Zeke? Your boss said Catherine was treating him."

Harry covered her joined hands at his waist with one of his own. "He was in rough shape, walking all the way from the claim to the Landing. But he ate a good dinner and slept through the night."

"And she knows to speak loud and clear?" she pressed.

"She knows. He's in good hands."

She leaned against him again. "So am I. Thank you for coming for me, Harry."

"I'll always come for you. I meant what I said. I love you, Katie Jo."

"I bet you say that to all the pretty gals," she said, but he could hear the teasing tone in her voice.

Harry squeezed her hands. "No, I don't. I haven't ever said it to any of the ladies I've courted. I don't think I loved them. I was fond of them, but it was like you said. They fit a picture in my head. You're so much more than that."

She nuzzled his back. "You know just what to say to turn a gal up sweet, Harry."

He chuckled. "I'm kind of glad that isn't true. I might have settled for filling out that picture, if it wasn't for you. Now, I have a chance for real happiness."

She sighed. He thought it was a pleased sound. He clucked to the horse to pick up its paces as Lancelot trotted out onto the path down to the Landing.

"What happens now?" she asked, as if she sensed their moment of privacy was growing short.

"Now, I get you back to the Landing, and you see about Zeke. I'll talk to Ciara. Maybe she'll let Jesse and me live at the inn for a time, so you and your brother can have our cabin."

She straightened away from him again. "What about the cabin on your claim?"

"It needs a bit more work," Harry said. "That storm the other night did some damage."

"We'll help you set it to rights," she promised. "Me and Zeke. We're used to doing for a claim."

"I'm not bringing you to the Landing so you can work," Harry protested. "Leastwise, not work for me. You know Ciara will welcome you if you want to work more for her."

"I might," she said. "Funny. I've been thinking about this day for years, the day Zeke and I left the claim to strike out on our own. I can hardly believe it's here. I have a lot of arrangements to make: where we'll live, how we'll make a living."

"I have a suggestion," Harry said.

"What?" she asked.

He reined in the horse, then slid from the saddle. Going down on one knee on the fir needle-strewn trail, he gazed up at her. "Katie Jo McAllister, you taught me how it should be between a husband and a wife, how they should share in the dreaming and the doing. You have the biggest heart of anyone I've ever met. I would be the luckiest man alive if you agreed to be my bride. Would you marry me?"

Her lips trembled. "Get me down."

He wasn't sure whether that was a joyous yes or a demanding no, but he lifted his arms and set her down beside him. She threw her arms about him and hugged him so tight the breath left his lungs.

"Yes, Harry," she murmured. "Yes, I will marry you and dream and do right beside you." She let go, then lifted her chin to press her lips against his. The kiss was certain, sweet, a promise of a life ahead of them.

As she pulled back, Harry caressed her cheek with one hand. Then he lifted her back onto the saddle with a feeling of pride and reverence. "Guess you know what you'll be doing, then."

"And Zeke?" she asked as he swung up in front of her.

"Zeke's welcome in our home as long as he wants."

She sighed and leaned against him. "Oh, Harry. I'm so happy."

He swore one of the buttons popped off his shirt as his chest swelled. "I'll do all I can to make sure you're always happy, darlin'."

"No one's always happy," she said as they set off for the Landing again. "But as long as we're together, every day will be a good day."

CHAPTER NINETEEN

THE RAIN BEGAN to fall, pattering down on the firs above them and dripping onto the path. Katie Jo didn't care. Even another windstorm couldn't have dampened her joy.

Harry Yeager loved her, and they were going to be married. The entire clearing of Wallin Landing seemed to glow as they rode in.

Ciara must have been watching from the inn, for she hurried out onto the back porch. "Katie Jo! Are you all right?"

"I'm better than all right," she said, as Harry reined in and swung down. He held up his arms, and she slid into his embrace. That smile said she never had to leave.

"Then your uncle let you go, for good?" Ciara pressed.

She made herself glance at the porch. "Yep. He knows I'm leaving, and I don't intend to come back. So, I'm all yours, if you want me."

Ciara clapped her hands. "You know I do! With you here, I can open for business six days a week sooner than I'd thought!"

"You'll have to get in line," Harry said, slipping one arm about her waist as he led her up under the shelter of the porch. "Katie Jo has agreed to marry me. She'll be a little busy helping me set up our home, just the way she wants it."

"Just the way *we* want it," Katie Jo corrected him, even as Ciara squealed and enveloped her in a hug.

"All this celebration comes at a price," Harry warned Ciara as they disengaged. "Katie Jo and Zeke need someplace to stay until we marry. I'd like to put them in Beth's old cabin. That means Jesse and I need somewhere to stay too. Can we bunk in the inn again for a short time?"

Ciara nodded. "I don't expect too many travelers as winter comes closer. You should be fine for a few weeks."

"Less than that," Harry said. "I'll talk with Levi this afternoon about holding the ceremony within the week. For now, we need to see how Zeke's fairing."

They found her brother still in the dispensary. Surrounded by all the bottles and boxes and bandages on the shelving, he still looked a little pale to her, but he was sitting on a chair next to Catherine's desk, and the pages in the nurse's book were full of tightly written notes.

"Katie Jo!" her brother greeted as they walked through the door. His green eyes brightened. "I knew Harry would rescue you."

"She rescued herself," Harry said with a wink to Katie Jo. "I just came along for the ride."

Zeke's smile flagged. "Then Uncle Cole will be coming after us?"

"No." The answer came from the door, where Drew now stood. He nodded to Harry and Katie Jo before crossing the room and bending to press a kiss to his wife's cheek. She smiled up at him.

Drew straightened and turned to Katie Jo and Zeke. "Your uncle has decided he'd be wiser to head north to the gold fields. Especially as three or four prospectors and loggers in the area also seem to think they paid to marry

Katie Jo. We explained she had other plans for her life, and none seemed disposed to argue with her."

Or at least to argue with Drew and his brothers.

"Thank you," Katie Jo said. "Thank you all."

"You're family," Drew said. "Family helps family." He nodded to Zeke. "Feeling better?"

"Yes, sir," Zeke said. "Good enough to join your logging crew."

Katie Jo stared at him.

Drew chuckled. "I'll see what I can do." He nodded around and left.

"Logging crew?" Katie Jo asked her brother.

"I want to do something no one else can do," he said, "but I'll settle for logging for now."

"After you're completely well," Catherine said firmly.

Katie Jo swallowed the lump that rose in her throat. "*Will* he get completely well?"

Catherine's face softened. "There's nothing to be done about his hearing, I'm afraid. The loss likely came from fevers when he was younger."

"He had a lot of those," Katie Jo remembered, giving her brother a commiserating look.

Catherine cocked her head. "I imagine he broke a few bones as well."

Katie Jo sighed. "Pert near every time he fell. Why, does that have something to do with his hearing too?"

"Not his hearing, but the weakness, body aches, and lack of appetite, certainly." She reached up and pulled down a slender volume. "According to Mrs. Child, your brother's symptoms closely match rickets."

Zeke grimaced. "What's that? Did something bite me, and I didn't know it?"

"No," Catherine said with a shake of her head. "It's brought on by lack of nourishment and want of fresh air."

Zeke glanced at Katie Jo. "My sister always fed me fine. I just didn't have the stomach to eat it."

"But you didn't have a lot of fresh air," Katie Jo countered. "Uncle thought it best you stay in bed when you were little. I suppose I just kept doing the same as you grew."

Catherine reached out a hand and patted hers. "You couldn't know. Many families fall prey to rickets. Thankfully, we know that exercise and the right foods can help put things to rights." She tapped the book on the desk. "Mrs. Child has some suggestions, but my father, who was a physician, recommended cod liver oil. Two doses a day to start, I should think."

Zeke grimaced again.

Katie Jo grabbed her brother's hand and squeezed. "That's easy, then. You'll be better in no time. Best news I've heard all day."

Harry coughed into his hand.

"Well, except for Harry saying he loved me and asking me to marry him," she said, cheeks heating.

That called for more congratulations and hugs all around.

"We'll need to make you a wedding dress," Catherine said, closing her journal as if she had discovered something more important to tend to. "Decorate the hall and the church. Bake for the reception."

Harry's eyes widened.

Katie Jo held up her hand. "I don't need any of that. Harry's fixing to talk to Pastor Wallin later today so we can be married as soon as possible. Harry loves me, just as I am."

He bent and kissed her cheek. "You know it, darlin'."

She could have lost herself in that tender look. Or found herself again.

"Well," Catherine said, smile hinting, "we can make you a veil at the very least. James has some lovely lace down at the mercantile. Harry or no Harry, every lady deserves something special on her wedding day."

Harry marveled at how quickly things changed at Wallin Landing over the next few days. Levi readily agreed to hold their wedding ceremony in the church in a week. In the meantime, Jesse packed up his and Harry's things and ported them back to the inn so Katie Jo and Zeke could set up in the old cabin along the trail. Catherine asked that Zeke eat at the inn for a time and coached Ciara and Katie Jo on the food he needed to grow stronger.

Every Wallin brother, Kit, Jesse, and Logan Bradshaw pitched in to help Harry and Katie Jo finish his cabin so she would be able to move in right after they wed. Working with Katie Jo, Nora even sewed curtains for the windows, and Catherine donated linens and a quilt from Mother Wallin for the bed.

No one had seen hide nor hair of Cole McAllister, which was all to the good. Katie Jo asked Harry to take her out to the claim later in the week with the wagon and a crate so she could fetch more things, including the chickens and a chest that had belonged to her mother. Harry had to chop through the fallen log first to clear the way.

"I suppose we'll just have to let the place lie empty," she told him as they loaded the last of the furnishings into the wagon to the squawk of confused chickens. "Zeke says he doesn't want it."

"You might be able to sell the claim," Harry ventured. "Folks are bound to move out this way sooner or later."

The other big change came on Wednesday, when Wallin Landing learned the results of its first school board election, which had been held the day before. Everyone had come to the schoolhouse to cast their votes during the day, and Rina and Dottie had counted them that evening.

"Catherine, John, and Kit are no surprise," Ciara said when Harry and Katie Jo arrived for dinner Wednesday night. Zeke had come over earlier to help Ciara with the extra work now that she was feeding eight instead of the four she'd originally planned. "But Mr. Bradshaw and Gladys Volland!"

Harry settled himself on the bench beside Katie Jo, leaving his former seat at the end of the table for her brother. "Should make for some interesting meetings."

Katie Jo glanced around. "Where's Alice? I'd like to hear what she thinks of this new board."

Ciara tipped her head toward the window. Outside on the porch, Alice and Jesse were in deep conversation. The little schoolteacher only reached to his collarbone, and Jesse had bent as if to drink in every word.

"Planning our trip to Seattle," Ciara said, laying a pan of biscuits down on the table. "We're going in tomorrow morning to fetch supplies and purchase some items for the school. You all are eating me out of house and home!"

"Not much longer," Harry promised, taking Katie Jo's hand and pressing a kiss against her fingers. Color climbed in her cheeks, and she gave him such a smile he could only bend closer and brush her lips with his as well.

Ciara sighed. "Just like Cinderella."

Katie Jo pulled back. "Cinder-who?"

"It's an old story," Ciara explained, "about a common girl who ended up marrying a prince."

Harry chuckled. "Then it doesn't apply to Katie Jo. If I'm a prince, it's only because I'm marrying a princess."

Ciara beamed. "And that's the way every groom should feel. Well done, Harry." She bustled back into the kitchen to help Zeke bring in the rest of the food.

"I'm not a princess," Katie Jo murmured in the

moment of quiet. "But you make me feel like a queen, Harry Yeager."

He kissed her fingers again. "Then let's go conquer a kingdom together, darlin'."

Thanks for reading Katie Jo and Harry's story. Harry followed a difficult road to find his true love, but I knew it was going to be Katie Jo long before he did. If you missed any of the Frontier Matches stories, or the stories about the Wallin clan, visit my website at *www.reginascott. com/frontierbachelors.html* for the full list.

Jesse Willets may have decided Alice Dennison is far beyond his reach, but a storm and a night in the woods may have something to say about the matter. Turn the page for a sneak peek of the next book in the Frontier Matches series, *The Schoolmarm's Convenient Marriage*.

SNEAK PEEK:

The Schoolmarm's Convenient Marriage

Book 4 in the Frontier Matches Series

Seattle, Washington Territory
October 1876

MUST A LADY travel to the ends of the Earth to gain command over her own future?

Apparently so, for Alice Dennison could only shake her head at the telegram gripped in her gloved hand.

"I hope it isn't bad news," her friend, Ciara Weatherly, said as they stood outside the telegraph office along the wharves. The shouts of the sailors offloading goods punctuated the whir of machinery at the nearby sawmill. Tar and cedar and brine mixed for a potent aroma under skies that hovered lower and darker every moment. Or maybe it was the words she'd read that had darkened her spirit.

THIS IS UNNECESSARY
RETURN AT ONCE

"Nothing that requires a reply," Alice said. "I'm sorry we delayed our visit to check."

"We always check when we come in for the mail." The voice rumbled from behind her, and she forced herself not to stiffen. Mr. Jesse Willets, who had driven them in to town, was a giant of a fellow, towering over everyone except Mr. Drew Wallin, who was apparently famous in the territory. Mr. Willets was also a man of few words. She had yet to determine whether it was because he had an economy of speech or because he simply knew few words.

"Then we have done our duty," she said. As they started forward, she crumpled the note and shoved it into her reticule to be summarily burned in the fire when they reached Wallin Landing.

That is, if she could remember how to rekindle the fire.

They had all been so patient with her, from Mrs. Rina Wallin, who was the lead teacher at the Lake Union School, to Alice's darling students, who ranged in age from four to seven. Rina had explained the expectations of Alice's role as schoolteacher, she had shown Alice how to clean and trim the lamps that lit her side of the two-room schoolhouse at the back of the village nestled along the shores of the lake, and she or one of the local gentlemen had repeatedly shown her how to lay the wood they brought her into the grate to keep the school warm as the autumn weather grew more brisk. She was the one who couldn't seem to get the wretched fire to stay lit!

She should have expected it would be a challenge to find her footing so far away from everything she'd once known, from everyone with whom she'd once thought to share her life. But she was more than ready to meet that challenge. Wallin Landing was her home now. She would do her best to be a good citizen, a good teacher, and a good friend. No more would she allow others to direct the course of her life, even if that meant remaining a spinster to the end of her days.

Ciara craned her neck to see into the bed of the wagon that had brought them to town, the breeze catching at her bonnet. Like Alice, she had dark hair, but hers seemed more easily tamed. Alice had neither the maid to help her or the time to pamper her hair here. So, she pulled it up and let it tumble down her back. So far, no one had protested.

"At least your things had come in," Ciara said. "Two crates of primers, six slates, and enough chalk to color Mount Rainier like a rainbow."

Alice's cheeks warmed, and again she chided herself. It was her classroom, and her choice of instruction. She did not have to ask anyone's approval.

For once.

"The children and I like to draw pictures," she explained. "I find it helps the learning process if they can visualize what we're discussing."

"I wish you'd been around when I was in school," Ciara said with a smile. She relaxed back beside her, chocolate-colored eyes brightening. "Now, to Kellogg's for my supplies."

Ciara was the proprietress of the Wooden Rose Inn, the first such establishment in the settlement. And it was flourishing thanks to her expertise in cooking. Another skill Alice lacked. But then, she hadn't been raised to cook and clean, merely manage those who did.

"Best we move fast," Mr. Willets said with a look to the sky.

Likely he was right. In Cawthorn, where she'd been raised, and in Boston, where she'd gone to a teacher's college, rains often came in the evenings with a sudden passion, then faded to leave everything fresh and clean. Here, rain spit and spat in a fussy little mist, often for several days in a row, before the sun came out as if opening its arms for an embrace. But the sky had been stingy today, threatening to pour but never letting go of a single drop.

"Then let's stop by the Pastry Emporium first," Ciara said. "I want you to meet my sister, Alice."

Frisco and Sutter, twin boys who attended the school and were in Rina's class, had made sure to tell Alice all about Ciara's famous older sister. Maddie O'Rourke Haggerty had opened the first and now the premiere bakery in Seattle.

"Everyone loves her cinnamon buns best," Sutter had said with a reverent lift of his blond brows.

"Her ginger snaps," his brother had insisted.

Sutter had shoved him in the chest. "Cinnamon buns."

"Ginger snaps!"

"Perhaps I'll see if I can bring back some of both," Alice had said, "for those who remember their manners."

They had instantly stood upright like tin soldiers and vowed to be complete gentlemen in her absence.

Now, Mr. Willets set his hands on Ciara's waist and boosted her onto the wagon's bench. Alice waited patiently for her turn. But the big logger seemed suddenly at odds. He shifted on his feet, and his gaze, a lighter gray than the sky, darted here and there like that of one of her students caught in an infraction.

"Is there a problem, Mr. Willets?" she asked, frowning.

"No." She could see his Adam's apple bob as he swallowed. Unlike many of the men in the area, he was clean shaven, the planes of his face firm and rather pleasant to look upon. His hair reminded her of the bark of the madrone tree she'd first seen in California, reddish brown and smooth. And his physique in the collarless flannel shirt and wool trousers could only be called impressive.

Not that a lady should notice such things.

Alice lifted her arms a little to encourage him. "I'm afraid I cannot climb up on my own, sir. Would you mind?"

He sighed as if she had asked him to perform the labors of Hercules, then set his hands on her waist. His fingers spanned the width, and suddenly she found it difficult to draw breath even though his touch was light. Then, *whoosh!* He all but tossed her up onto the bench as if the momentary contact with her had burned him. She clutched at Ciara to keep from falling into her friend's lap.

"Are you in such a hurry, Jesse?" Ciara asked with a frown as she helped Alice right herself.

The third overskirt on her gown snagged on a splinter of wood, and she had to tug the blue-sprigged material free. She'd thought she'd chosen such practical gowns when she'd stolen away in the middle of the night to catch the train west, but the silks and linens of summer had proven impractical here. As soon as she started drawing her salary, she would commission something more useful. Wool. No overskirts. No lace.

This time she was the one who sighed.

But she kept a smile on her face as Mr. Willets climbed up beside them and drove them up the hill to Second Avenue, where Mrs. Haggerty had her bakery.

"I see a crowd has already gathered," she told Ciara as the wagon drew next to the boardwalk. "Testimony to your sister's skills, no doubt."

But Ciara wasn't smiling, and Alice realized why. No lamps glowed inside the bakery. Someone had affixed a large sign, hastily scrawled by the look of the lettering, on the big front window, proclaiming the establishment closed. Several men were clustered around, muttering.

"Maddie never closes except on Sundays," Ciara said, voice trembling. "Even when she came out for my wedding, she baked ahead and had someone keep the shop open. Take me to Fourth Avenue, Jesse. I need to see my family."

Jesse nodded. Family came first. He'd heard his father say that many a time, and he believed it. He urged the horses around the corner and up the steep hill for Fourth, where many of the nicer houses had been built.

Ciara pointed out which one belonged to her sister, but he thought he might have guessed. Like many of the sweets Maddie Haggerty baked, the roof dripped with curlicues like icing.

"Stay here," Ciara said as he reined in the horses, "until I know who's sick and with what." She clambered over Miss Dennison and scrambled down before Jesse could come around to help her.

Leaving him sitting with the schoolmarm.

He stayed on his side of the bench.

She stayed on hers.

"I do hope no one is terribly ill," she murmured in a voice that the songbirds must envy. That was the thing with Alice Dennison. Everything about her was dainty and sweet, from the shiny black hair that tumbled down behind her back like an obsidian waterfall, to her delicately featured face and the slender figure her fancy clothes outlined. Even her hands fluttered like little birds. Next to her, Jesse felt like a giant.

A great, lumbering, not-too-bright giant.

"Probably just took a chill," he managed.

Immediately she turned her gaze to his. She had eyes like the purple-blue violas his sisters liked to pick in the summer, and they too often brimmed with tears that could make a man promise anything to see her smile again.

"Do you think so?" she breathed.

"Sure," he said. He caught his balance and realized he'd slid as far as dignity allowed to his side of the bench.

"Have you a great deal of experience with such things?" she asked, and there was no skepticism in her tone, only a wide-eyed wonder. "Some training as a physician?"

"Nope," Jesse said. "Only nine little brothers and sisters."
Now her lashes were fluttering too. "Nine!"

Did she think that a good thing? A bad thing? He'd met folks in both camps. Not that it mattered. He wouldn't have traded any of his brothers or sisters, for all each of them had given him a bad time or two along the way. In fact, he'd once dared to hope he might have a parcel of young'uns of his own. That hope dimmed with each passing year. Too few women, too many expectations.

Her delicate black brow drew together, and so did his stomach. "I don't believe I've met any of them," she said. "Do they attend the school?"

"My family lives in Olympia." There. A full sentence with subject and verb. Ma would be so proud. He could hear her in his head.

You're a fine man, Jesse. You're kind and sensible, and you don't use that height and strength of yours to bully. You have no reason to be bashful.

"Olympia," she said, brow clearing. "Yes, the town at the southern end of Puget's Sound. It is the territorial capital and the third city incorporated in the territory."

She sounded as if she were reciting from a book. He knew the same facts, but Olympia meant far more to him than that. It was the wind rippling the grasses on the prairie, the splash of a salmon leaping out of the bay. It was the laughter of his brothers and sisters as they hunted the woods for blackcaps, the moo of contented dairy cows. So, he just nodded.

"I would very much like to see it someday," she said. "Perhaps you'd care to share your experiences there."

The memories evaporated from his mind, leaving nothing but a wall of white broader than Rainier's glaciers. That had ever been his problem. He'd never been the center of attention in his family. He didn't know how to deal with it when strangers focused on him. Would he sound as if he were bragging? Would he sound illiterate?

He was just thankful to see Ciara returning, hands fisted in her skirts.

Until she spoke.

"Leave," she said, voice once more trembling. "Go back to the Landing. Tell Kit I'll be home when I can."

"Oh, Ciara!" Miss Dennison cried, reaching out a hand toward her. "What is it?"

"They're not sure," Ciara admitted with a glance back to the house, "and I haven't been inside yet, so you are both safe. My brother-in-law Michael spoke to me through the glass on the front window. Maddie's sick, and he fears it's smallpox."

Jesse's grip on the reins tightened, and Lancelot protested. He forced his hands to relax even as his mind whirled. He'd never lived through a smallpox epidemic, but his parents told stories of the fast-moving disease. Its rash could disfigure, even kill! Was Ciara's family safe? Was his?

Miss Dennison must have heard of the disease as well, for she clutched the sideboard, and he could only hope she wasn't feeling faint.

"Oh, no!" she cried. "I heard a rumor of it when I came through San Francisco last month, but I was hoping that was all it was, a rumor."

"We don't know yet," Ciara cautioned. "But I can't leave them. And I don't dare bring it home to baby Grace. Tell Kit I love him."

Now her body was trembling. So was Miss Dennison's. Jesse raised his head. He was strong, he was healthy. It was his duty to help others who might be affected.

"We will," Miss Dennison promised. "Please, be careful."

Ciara nodded. And all Jesse could do was start the horses forward.

"How horrid," Miss Dennison said, voice small and frightened as they headed for the road out to Wallin Landing. "Of course we must carry her words to her dear husband and baby. I will pray for her safety and the health of her sister and her family."

Jesse nodded. He'd pray too. Not out loud with a lot of words. God didn't expect that, and he was forever grateful for the fact.

Seattle was pushing ever outward, but they soon reached the trees that marked the edge. The schoolmarm fell silent as they drove under the canopy of trees that lined the road out to the Landing. It was cooler here, but it wasn't just the overlapping branches of fir and cedar. The temperature was dropping. A storm was coming. He just had to get them to the Landing before it hit.

He slapped down the reins. "Lancelot! Percival! Yah!"

"Lancelot and Percival?" she asked, voice sounding brittle, as if she was searching for anything to talk about besides the danger they were fleeing.

"The horses," he clarified.

"Named for the knights of King Arthur's court? How marvelous! Are they yours, Mr. Willets?"

She *was* new. "Mr. Wallin's. He allows the use of them."

"Which Mr. Wallin?" she asked. He was relieved when she continued speaking as if answering her own question. "Not Mr. Drew Wallin—he is your employer. I believe Mr. Simon Wallin has horses, but they would be needed at the farm so I doubt he could allow others to use them on a regular basis. Mr. James Wallin, the owner of the mercantile, perhaps?"

Jesse grinned at her. "That's right."

She stared at him, and his smile faded. What had he done wrong now?

She dropped her gaze, fiddled with the little beaded sack in her lap. A shiver went through her.

Well, of course, Jesse. If you noticed the cold in your flannels, what do you think she feels in that frilly dress?

"Extra blanket in the bed," he offered.

She twisted and glanced around, then pulled up the

thick wool he had packed before they'd headed out that morning. "How very wise of you to think to bring this."

Once again, she was making him feel clever. But the weather mocked him, daring him to try to make the run. The trees were starting to talk, swaying and gossiping in breathy rustles as the wind picked up. In the distance, he thought he heard a rumble.

Lancelot and Percival picked up their paces, as if they had heard it too and longed for the safety of their barn.

"I suppose some would say we should have stayed in town," she ventured, wrapping the blanket around her shoulders. "With the weather and the lack of a chaperone. But we are out of doors and in easy view of anyone along the road."

The West Lake Road had become more widely traveled over the years as more folks filed claims along the hillside above David Denny's. But anyone with any sense would be heading into town this afternoon, not out.

The trees began to whip in earnest, and the first lightning bolt flashed across the sky above their tops. She cried out and hunched closer to him, eyes wide. Lancelot tossed his head at the noise.

Best thing he could do for them all was keep calm.

"Rain's coming," he said. "Put that blanket up over your head."

She started to do as he'd bid, but she unfolded the blanket further, then flipped it up over his head too. He smiled at her thoughtfulness.

Ahead, with a mighty creak of protest, one of the firs toppled.

Lancelot reared in his traces, and Jesse clung to the reins, fighting for control. Thunder roared, shaking the wagon. Both horses shuddered. And then the rain started, sluicing out of the clouds. More branches began dropping on either side of them.

Miss Dennison didn't scream. She didn't tremble.

She just looked at him with her great purple-blue eyes brimming and said, "Please, Mr. Willets, can you save us?"

Jesse raised his head, pulling the blanket partially off her ebony hair. "Yes, ma'am. You can count on me."

Learn more at
www.reginascott.com/schoolmarm.html.

OTHER BOOKS BY REGINA SCOTT

Frontier Bachelors/Frontier Matches
The Bride Ship (Allegra and Clay)
Would-Be Wilderness Wife (Catherine and Drew)
Frontier Engagement (Rina and James)
Instant Frontier Family (Maddie and Michael)
A Convenient Christmas Wedding (Nora and Simon)
Mail-Order Marriage Promise (Dottie and John)
His Frontier Christmas Family (Callie and Levi)
Frontier Matchmaker Bride (Beth and Hart)
The Perfect Mail-Order Bride (Ada and Scout)
Her Frontier Sweethearts (Ciara and Kit)

American Wonders Collection
A Distance Too Grand
Nothing Short of Wondrous
A View Most Glorious

Fortune's Brides Series
Never Doubt a Duke
Never Borrow a Baronet
Never Envy an Earl
Never Vie for a Viscount
Never Kneel to a Knight
Never Marry a Marquess
Always Kiss at Christmas
It Started With a Duke (Collection)
Never Pursue a Prince
Never Court a Count
Never Romance a Rogue
Never Love a Lord
Never Beguile a Bodyguard

Grace-by-the-Sea Series
The Matchmaker's Rogue
The Heiress's Convenient Husband
The Artist's Healer
The Governess's Earl
The Lady's Second-Chance Suitor
The Siren's Captain

Uncommon Courtships Series
The Unflappable Miss Fairchild
The Incomparable Miss Compton
The Irredeemable Miss Renfield
The Unwilling Miss Watkin
An Uncommon Christmas
The Uncommon Courtships Series (Collection)

Lady Emily Capers
Secrets and Sensibilities
Art and Artifice
Ballrooms and Blackmail
Eloquence and Espionage
Love and Larceny
Dangerous Dalliances (First two books and exclusive novella)
Perilous Passions (Last three books)

Marvelous Munroes Series
My True Love Gave to Me
The Rogue Next Door
The Marquis' Kiss
A Match for Mother
The Marvelous Munroes Series (Collection)

Spy Matchmaker Series
The Husband Mission
The June Bride Conspiracy

The Heiress Objective
The Spy Matchmaker Series (Collection)

The Regent's Devices Trilogy (writing as R.E. Scott with Shelley Adina)
The Emperor's Aeronaut
The Prince's Pilot
The Lady's Triumph

About the Author

REGINA SCOTT STARTED writing novels in the third grade. Thankfully for literature as we know it, she didn't sell her first novel until she learned a bit more about writing. Since her first book was published, her stories have traveled the globe, with translations in many languages including Dutch, German, Italian, and Portuguese. She now has more than sixty-five published works of warm, witty romance, and more than 1 million copies of her books are in reader hands.

While she adores the elegance of the Regency period in England and has penned many stories set then, she loves getting to write about history closer to her home in the Puget Sound area of Washington State, where she lives with her husband. She also loves diving into history headfirst. She has dressed as a Regency dandy, driven four-in-hand, learned to fence, and sailed on a tall ship, all in the name of research, of course. Learn more about her at www.reginascott.com.

9 7 9 8 9 8 6 5 7 9 0 5 4